BEACH

A QUILTING COZY MYSTERY

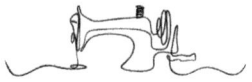

Kathryn Mykel

The book inside the books

Copyright © 2025 by Kathryn Mykel/Kathryn LeBlanc

All rights reserved. No part of this book may be reproduced in any form or by any electronic or mechanical means, including information storage and retrieval systems, without written permission from the author, except for the use of brief quotations in a book review. This is a work of fiction. Names, characters, places, and incidents either are the products of the author's imagination or are used fictitiously. Any resemblance to actual persons, living or dead, events, or locales is entirely coincidental.

Edited by Sharp Eyed Shari
Formatted by Kathryn LeBlanc

blurb

When a quilting group heads to the local beach for a relaxing seaside retreat, the last thing they expect is to be caught in a deadly confrontation. But when a local finds a dead body after a heated brawl, all fingers point to the quilting ladies. The problem? Each quilter is the other's alibi, but they all have motive.

Enter Detective Reggie Thistlewitt, a sharp investigator. When everyone looks guilty, how will he tell who's really pulling the strings?

Perfect for fans of amateur sleuths, this beachy whodunit will keep you guessing until the final stitch is sewn!

Beach Brawl *was first mentioned in Quilting Calamity, and is found hinted at throughout many of author Kathryn Mykel's other cozies.*

This is the book that her main characters are reading within the books.

CHAPTER 1
stitches and suitcases

The shells of the Cape Cod driveway popped under her wheels like nature's bubble wrap. Cara Abbott cut the engine and swung open the Jeep's door. A rush of salt air swept in, mercifully clearing out the lingering lavender spray and burnt coffee. She coughed, then laughed at herself.

"This is it?" Bean leaned forward from the back seat, her wild red curls flopping into Cara's face. "It's even cuter than the photos! And I didn't think that was possible."

"It's the same one we rented last year." Cara shook her head.

"I still think it's better than the photographs, and my condo."

"You live less than five miles away." Trudy giggled.

Perched on Sand Dollar Beach, the weathered blue cottage, with its white shutters and wraparound porch, looked like it had stepped straight off the pages of a summer novel. For Cara and her quilting crew, its nearness to home made it feel less like a rental and more like theirs.

In the passenger seat, Haze folded her arms. "Windows look secure. No visible water damage *this time*."

"High praise," Marnie said, already out of the car.

Trudy exited next, clutching a pie carrier in both hands. "I brought lemon custard for later."

"Is it a bribe for the first pick of rooms?" Bean called untangling herself from the back seat.

Laughing, Trudy responded, "No, but now I regret not making two."

Cara jumped out and popped the trunk. Unloading, she helped with the quilting totes, sewing machines, and bins of fabric.

They didn't pack light.

"You can't have a beachside quilting retreat on charm alone." Bean chirped.

As Cara reached for her favorite notions pouch, something small clattered to the ground. She bent to retrieve it —a silver charm bracelet. Her own! The tiny scissor charm sparkled in the sunlight.

"Get it together, Abbott," she whispered, clipping it back onto her wrist. "This is supposed to be relaxing."

A rogue wave crashed against the shore, infusing the air with salty spray. Just then, Cara's quilting bag, half-unzipped, toppled onto the sandy path to the house. She lurched forward instinctively and her basket of precut fabric squares wobbled dangerously close to disaster.

"Watch it!" Bean yelped behind her.

Geez, that would've taken hours to sort again had they toppled out.

Cara turned to see Bean awkwardly hopping backward, one foot covered in sand, the other kicking up dried seaweed as she pointed at the culprit. "I thought it was a jellyfish!"

I thought she was worried about my fabric!

Cara used the toe of her sandals to kick up the culprit. "It's not a jellyfish, just a half-buried flip-flop." Cara chortled. She hadn't expected her quilting escape to start with a scream. She chuckled to herself nervously. "Well, aren't we a pair today?"

She brushed off Bean's pants, and the breeze tousled her silver bob, her mismatched earrings—thimble and flamingo—swaying with the motion. "A wet *fat quarter* would be an interesting way to start the weekend," Cara teased. For all the angst of getting there—this was familiar. Fabric in hand, feet in the sand, and friends, mostly friendly.

Bean leaned close. "It's going to be okay, you know. We're going to stitch things back together. You'll see."

"I hope so," Cara replied. They were all hauling baggage—some of it literal, some not.

The other middle-aged women brushed past the dune grass along the path to the house and ahead of Bean and Cara.

Sun, sea, and stitching. How bad can it be?

She paused at the porch, hesitant.

Inside, muffled voices carried, sharp and strained.

Conflict already?

"You shouldn't have said that," came Marnie's unmistakable bravado.

"Well, someone had to," Trudy replied sharply, her tone shrill and piercing in the tranquil air.

"You're not exactly innocent, Trudy," Marnie snapped. "Want me to bring up the boutique investment?"

Trudy hissed a reply that Cara couldn't make out—then a loud *thud* of luggage cut the conversation short. She filed the words away for later: *Boutique investment?*

"This retreat is sure to be good therapy, but with better snacks," Bean said, charging ahead of Cara and into the house without an inkling of the trouble brewing inside.

The screen door ricocheted on its hinges with a *snap*, nearly clipping Cara. She opened the door just as Trudy whirled past with an exaggerated smile. Her soft, puffed-up strawberry-blonde curls bobbed.

"Everything okay?"

"I was just getting the fridge ready!" Trudy chimed, her voice now syrupy sweet and her bright blue eyes wide and innocent.

Marnie had followed Trudy out of the open kitchen. The whole living area was a spacious open concept. "Peachy," Marnie snapped, her smile as brittle as an old spool of thread. Wearing a bold-patterned tunic, she had her espresso-brown hair twisted into a no-nonsense knot, her lipstick fierce, and her eyebrows sharper than her tone. She dragged her leopard-print luggage and a visible storm cloud. "It only took two minutes to fall into old habits."

What does that mean?

The beach house was cozy. Nautical-themed artwork hung slightly crooked on the paneled walls. The open living space had multiple seating areas, charming woven rugs, and windows that opened wide to let in the sea air. A long wooden table—clearly meant for seafood boils or jigsaw puzzles—would now become part of "quilting central."

Bean flopped her wiry frame onto the couch, oblivious, or pretending to be, and kicked off her sandals. Her pastel tie-dye shirt read: *Stitch Happens,* and a salsa stain bloomed proudly above the words. Her frizzy red curls had escaped from her sun hat. "I call this sewing spot. Natural light, full breeze, and a perfect view of the snack table."

"I wish I could eat like you and stay thin as a rail," Trudy said to Haze, the last one to enter the cottage.

Haze set a plastic case of color-coded charm packs on the nearest surface. Her sleek black bob didn't move an inch, but her eyes scanned the room like a general assessing terrain, complete with an overly arched brow. "But that couch will be terrible for your posture."

"I'm doing creative visualization. I brought my entire beach scene appliqué kit. It's going to be 'sew' great!" Bean's voice echoed off the walls.

"Well I'm doing damage control," Marnie grumbled, rifling through her tote. "Where's my lint roller? Everything smells like Trudy's lavender dryer sheets."

"They're calming," Trudy retorted, then muttered under her breath. "Unlike all of you."

"It'll be 'sew' great, only if you don't use those ridiculous colors again." Haze cast a sideways glance at Bean. Petite and perfectly pressed, Haze wore linen pants. A wristband with printed measuring increments peeked from beneath the sleeve of her matching top.

"Better than your haunted quilt of doom," Marnie spouted.

"Ooh, my Nightmare on Quilt Street project," Haze chimed in, smirking. "At least I finished it!" she shot back, her tone playful yet edged with a hint of defensiveness.

Cara forced a smile, but something inside her itched. A familiar worry: five friends, one bathroom, and too much history. She loved them all fiercely, but ever since the last guild meeting—and the blowout over the quilt show judging—things had been off.

"I'll make tea," she offered, mostly to buy herself a moment.

The women went right to work setting up folding tables. Cara half-heartedly listened as the others went through the motions of organizing their space, and she went to the sink, filled the pot, then set it on the stove to boil.

"—no way he'll be around. He doesn't even know we're here."

"I heard he still lurks around the dunes with that stupid metal detector. Runs the entire length of the beach."

"One 'accidental' rotary cutter slip and he'll think twice." Marnie's snarl caught Cara's attention.

That's harsh! Even for Darryl Cunningham.

The name buzzed in her mind like a nagging mosquito. The man was a parasite—once part of their guild, though he wasn't ever really a quilter, now persona non grata. A professional pot stirrer if ever there was one, especially with Marnie. Tension brewed, just like the tea kettle, whenever he was around.

She pulled out a mismatched set of nautical-themed mugs and an organic jar of honey from the cupboard just as the teapot began to whistle. She filled the mugs and stirred in the honey before passing them out.

"To a peaceful weekend," she said, leaning against the armrest of the couch in the living room area beside Bean and raising her cup. The sunlight streamed through enormous ocean-facing windows draped with wispy sheer curtains. *A perfect place to quilt.*

Everyone mimed clinking mugs, some more earnestly than others, and Cara detected a flicker of movement outside the window. He leaned against the old driftwood post that marked the edge of the dunes.

The town's resident creep, professional nuisance, and patchwork pretender—was watching them from the beach. His mirrored sunglasses hid his eyes but his gaze, like sand in a shoe, was uncomfortable and unavoidable nonetheless.

"He's back," Cara groaned.

"No." Bean glanced up from the bag of supplies. "It's like we manifested him."

Cara scoffed. "Lurking like a hermit crab without a shell."

Marnie swore under her breath, and Trudy made a sound of disgust.

"Ignore him," Haze said. "He's probably looking for change under the seaweed again."

"I can't stand that guy," Bean uttered an exasperated groan, her nose wrinkling. "Always sniffing around for trouble. What's he doing out there, anyway?"

She twisted around, kneeling on the couch cushions and peered dramatically over the back of it. The others gathered too, peeking through the window like curious cats.

"He's probably just beachcombing," Trudy offered unconvincingly. "He lives around here, doesn't he?"

Marnie crossed her arms and glared toward the window. "Like a barnacle. Hard to scrape off."

"Or a rash," Cara added.

"Maybe he's just looking for inspiration," Bean suggested, chipper as ever sliding back around. "He could start his own Beach Trash Sampler quilt."

The women laughed, but the edge remained. Cara's gaze lingered on Darryl's reflection, twin suns glinting back from his glasses, and she shut the curtain.

"He could make a quilt of dirty old fishing nets," Marnie said, her voice laced with mockery.

Bean rummaged around in her bags. "I brought my

famous shrimp salad!" she announced, striking a mock-ta-da pose with the Tupperware and a serving spoon held high above in her insulated tote. "It's a hit at every retreat!"

Haze nudged Marnie. "As long as it's not the same recipe she used last time."

Bean's cheeks flushed, but she giggled it off. "Okay, so maybe I've refined it a little since then. What do you think this is—*The Great British Bake Off*?"

Cara went to the cupboards again and pulled out the dinner ware. The playful jabs masked deeper issues. *I'm torn. I want to laugh, but I also wish I could pull everyone aside for a heart-to-heart.*

Once dinner was set up, Cara piled heaping helpings onto her plate but only picked at her food. She spied Darryl outside the window several more times until he was right outside a now-open window.

"Hey, quilters!" he shouted. "Hope you're not expecting too much peace and quiet. This is my beach, too, you know."

"We're just here to quilt, not to stir up your seaweed. Go away." Marnie tugged at her scarf with exasperation, her bangle bracelets clinking in protest.

"Ignore him," Cara said, rising and going to the window before snapping it shut on the interloper. "Let's just finish dinner so we can get to quilting. Remember, we're here to enjoy ourselves!"

Marnie cleared the dishes while Bean fluffed pillows on the couch like she was preparing for a slumber party no one had RSVP'd to.

"We should do the picnic tomorrow," Trudy said, dabbing her mouth with a lavender colored napkin and breaking the silence. "Get out there before the sun gets too hot. I brought the bamboo utensils and that pineapple-shaped board."

Cara nodded absently. "It'll be nice to be outside after a late night of sewing. If he's not lurking, that is."

"Oh, you can bet he'll be around," Haze said bluntly, wiping her hands on a dish towel as she turned from the sink. "But we'll bring our quilts and set up our territory."

"I can hand-stitch and glare at the same time," Bean chimed in.

Palms together, Trudy tapped her fingers together as her planning continued, "Let's aim for early afternoon. We'll have a morning full of quilting and I'll prepare the lemonade and snacks tonight before I go to bed."

"I'll prepare a warning look for Darryl," Marnie retorted. "And if he gets too close, he'll get a fat quarter slap."

Cara laughed softly, but her eyes lingered on the storm-darkening horizon through the window. "Just keep it light. Quilting and snacks, no drama."

But as the evening wore on, it became increasingly clear that this retreat, meant to be a peaceful escape, was rife with buried conflicts, and she was unsure whether or not to intervene. Cara excused herself. "I just need a few minutes to let my dinner settle." She snatched an old Storm at Sea quilt from the couch and brought it out with her to the porch swing.

The sun slipped below the horizon, bleeding gold and orange into the darkening blue ocean. From the corner of her eye, she spotted Darryl again. *Watching us. Creep!*

He called out, "You making quilts or just a mess?"

Just then Marnie stepped onto the porch and shouted, "Go sew yourself Darryl."

Darryl smirked, waving his metal detector around, and ignored her.

"I swear that contraption is just an excuse to be meddlesome," Marnie said to Cara.

CHAPTER 2

batting down trouble

The next afternoon, Cara spotted the metal detector before she saw the man. That ridiculous hum—part mosquito, part menace—buzzed louder than the incoming tide.

"Nope," she muttered to herself, adjusting the corner of the picnic quilt like nothing was wrong. "Not today, Darryl."

The scent of saltwater clung to the breeze, mingling with sunscreen, sliced watermelon, and the sharp edge of dread.

The others hadn't noticed him yet. Trudy was too busy reorganizing the finger sandwiches by triangle orientation. Haze was testing wind direction for optimal quilt stability. And Marnie was arguing with Bean about whether tie-dye should be allowed on a beach-themed quilt.

Cara was on the fence about the tie-dye as she smoothed the huge king-size quilt again, this time with a little more force. She plopped her book down in one of the corners. If Darryl Cunningham was back to sniff around, their peaceful retreat was about to unravel faster than Bean's free-motion quilting.

"Perfect spot for a light early dinner, Cara!" Trudy exclaimed after setting up the food, then plopped down beside her.

Cara leaned back onto her elbows and glanced across the quilt. There were cloth napkins with little palm trees embroidered by Trudy. Five chilled lemonade jars nestled in a wine cooler disguised as a basket, next to a pineapple-shaped charcuterie board. *Of course the crackers are organized by grain.* Someone—probably Haze—had placed a small squeeze bottle of hand sanitizer between the grapes and the baby carrots.

It was all too curated and too perfect for Cara. Especially for a bunch of women, all seasoned by life and fabric stashes, trying to cling to a version of peace that didn't involve drama, whispers, and backstabbing.

Trudy began humming "Under the Boardwalk," and Bean swatted at a horsefly with one of the napkins. "Nasty things."

"This is lovely," Cara finally replied.

Trudy unpacked snacks from her tidy, monogrammed lunch tote. Her soft curls bounced with every movement, and her smile was brighter than the foil-wrapped cookies she had absolutely baked herself.

"Nothing like a bit of ocean breeze to inspire our creativity," Trudy said, nibbling on a cookie.

Or a nap!

Trudy offered one to Cara.

"Yes, I agree," Cara replied, her smile faltering. She accepted a cookie without really looking at it; but she knew it would be delicious, knowing Trudy. Cara unwrapped a sandwich—white bread, no crust cut into a perfect triangle. *No surprise there.* "Let's hope the only thing we have to worry about is keeping the seagulls away."

As if summoned by spite instead of breadcrumbs, a cacophony of squawks sliced through the air. Cara glanced up, expecting flapping wings—but found something far more unsettling.

What's he doing here?

Standing at the edge of their picnic was none other than Darryl Cunningham, a local with a penchant for trouble. His silhouette was unmistakable—tanned skin like tough leather, filthy cargo shorts, and that same smug stance like he'd found something valuable just by being difficult. His mirrored sunglasses caught the sun and hid whatever sleaze lurked behind them.

"Look what the tide dragged in," Darryl called out, a smirk plastered on his face. "The Quilting Queens, setting up shop on a beach! I hope you're not planning to sew any of your dirty laundry out here."

Cara's stomach knotted as she exchanged glances with the others. Bean paused mid-bite on a peanut butter granola bar, crumbs stuck to her cheek like accidental freckles. Marnie's face flushed, and she crossed her arms defensively while Haze shot Cara a *What now?* look.

"Just enjoying a little retreat, Darryl," Cara said, tugging one of her mismatched earrings—a tiny felt tomato pin cushion this time—and tucking her hair behind her ear like it might help her listen for an escape hatch. "What brings you here?"

"Oh, you know me," he drawled, taking a step closer. "Just combing the beach for treasures. But it's hard to treasure anything when you've got a bunch of old secrets flapping around like your quilting scraps."

Marnie's eyes narrowed. "Is that supposed to mean something, or are you just bad at metaphors?" Her tone was razor-sharp, matching the angle of her immaculately sculpted brows.

Darryl chuckled, his eyes glinting with mischief. "I hear things. Rumors float through our little town like driftwood. Secrets from all those late-night quilting bees. Maybe I should start sharing what I know."

A hush fell over the group. They'd left their condos and small Cape-style homes behind, pooling together to rent a large waterfront house for the weekend—and the chance to sew together under one roof. Instead, Darryl's voice carried the weight of their whole town. Even here, away from familiar neighborhoods, he'd found a way to taint it.

"Now's not the time for games, Darryl," Cara warned, but her voice was drowned out by crashing waves.

"Oh, I think it is," he sneered, stepping forward. "Who

would want to be the subject of the next scandal? Just think of the headlines: *Quilting Queens Unraveled!*"

Darryl's taunts triggered a spark in Bean. *Wait, no, it was Marnie.* Cara was off her game. *Who can blame me when Darryl is acting like the ghost of Guild-Dramas Past.* "You think you can just walk up here and threaten us? You don't know a thing about us!"

"Care to prove me wrong?" he retorted, his tone dripping with condescension. "Or should I start spilling? I mean, what about that little mishap at last year's quilting contest, Bean? Or Cara's little run-in with the law? You ladies have been coming out to the beach for nearly as long as I have."

"That was a misunderstanding!" Cara shot back, her hands clenched into fists. *One bad parking lot incident involving an overzealous meter maid and a quilt display is not a "run-in with the law."*

Marnie straightened, face reddening with anger. "How dare you!" Marnie pushed back in her chair and jumped to her feet. She charged at Darryl, shoving him hard in the chest. "You're nothing but a lowlife! Leave us alone!"

Darryl stumbled but quickly regained his footing, his expression a mix of surprise and delight. "Feisty, aren't we?" he taunted, raising his hands mockingly. "Come on, ladies! Let's see what you've got!"

The beach erupted as the other quilters stood, ready to defend their dignity. Horribly, a full-blown argument ensued. Haze stepped in, her voice cool as a cucumber.

"This is exactly what he wants," she said, trying to separate her friend from this man, but chaos reigned.

Adrenaline coursed through Cara's veins, and she grabbed Marnie's arm, tugging her back as she stepped between the quilters and Darryl.

"Stop it! You're giving him exactly what he wants!" Cara pleaded, but the atmosphere was electric, and she couldn't help but worry about where it was all heading.

Darryl, seeing his audience dissipate, scoffed and backed off, muttering under his breath. "You'll regret this. I'll be watching." With that, he stalked away, leaving a tense silence in his wake.

As the dust settled—on the sand—the group stood there in a circle, faces flushed and each of them breathing heavily. An uneasy knot tightened in Cara's stomach. "Are we really going to let him get to us like that?"

"We can't let him walk all over us," Marnie snapped, still trembling with rage. "We have every right to be here."

"But his words hit a nerve," Cara admitted, glancing at each of her friends. "He knows things."

Bean stared at the tide, lips moving like she was rehearsing a defense. Trudy pretended to rummage in the cooler, but her hands trembled just enough for the ice cubes to rattle.

As the sun began to dip toward the horizon line, painting the sky in stormy hues, Cara glanced out at the tumultuous ocean. The sea roared, a mirror to their growing unease and the sinking realization that this retreat was not going to be the peaceful escape she had hoped for.

"Let's just try to enjoy our evening," Cara suggested, but her voice lacked conviction. "We came here to quilt and relax, didn't we?"

Back at their beach house, the quilters bent over their projects, the only sounds were the anxious hum of sewing machines and the restless cicadas in the background.

Even Bean, usually a chatterbox during their sewing sessions, focused on a fiddly section of appliqué with uncharacteristic concentration. Her tongue darted in and out in rhythm with her needle.

Cara stood at the pressing station, mashing a stack of half-square triangles into submission, steam hissing from the iron.

"Need a new iron?" Haze asked without glancing up. Her tone was dry, but Cara didn't miss the undercurrent —*I'm pressing too hard*.

"This one's fine," Cara replied. The problem wasn't the iron. It was the somber mood.

Across the room, Marnie ripped out a seam for the third time. "If that man shows up again, I'm going to—"

"Baste him into a corner?" Trudy offered gently. She was assembling the rows of her quilt. "Violence won't help. We're already unnerved."

"Speak for yourself," Marnie shot back, brandishing her tiny seam ripper like a serious weapon.

"What I don't get is how he knows so much about us?" Bean asked, her voice uncharacteristically small. "It's like he knows my thread snapped in the corner of the binding on my last show quilt . . . and that I glued it."

Everyone froze.

"You glued your binding down?" Haze asked, horrified.

"No," Bean said, defensively. "Just the corner. I was desperate. Okay, fine—I was being lazy. After all that hard work and those final stitches, I said the heck with it. It's not the end of the world."

"Darryl couldn't know that," Cara said kindly.

Bean nodded, still flushed. "I know. But it seems like he knows all of our secrets."

They stitched for a beat, each woman lost in her own thoughts, needles thumping but mouths firmly shut.

Cara drifted back to her cutting mat to trim her stack of blocks and said, "I feel like he's trying to divide us, but I don't know why."

"Too late," Trudy whispered. "We're already frayed at the seams."

Bean sighed, dramatically flinging her appliqué block onto the table. "Okay. Enough with the secret-keeping bad juju energy. Darryl doesn't know anything unless we give him power. He's just a sunburnt man with a metal detector and too much time on his hands."

"And chafing," Marnie added. "I hope he has chafing."

That earned a few chuckles. Even Haze cracked a reluctant smile.

"We can't let one crusty barnacle ruin our entire retreat," Cara deadpanned, brushing threads from her lap. "We came here to quilt and have fun, didn't we?"

At that, Trudy gave a satisfied little gasp and held up her finished quilt top. "Well, *I* came here to finish this—and I did!"

The group paused, then Bean leapt up and applauded. "Show us, show us! Parade it around!"

Trudy stood proudly, holding out the mini quilt—a cheerful composition of pastel Dresden fans bordered with tiny prairie points. "It's called *Sunset Breeze*."

"Now that's a beach finish," Cara said, rising to admire the points. "Perfect."

"Less talk," Marnie said, standing and stretching. "More marshmallows. I say we build a bonfire on the beach and celebrate like we mean it."

Haze arched a brow. "*You* brought marshmallows?"

"*I* brought *everything*," Trudy beamed. "Chocolate, jumbo marshmallows, graham crackers, even the skewers."

"Good another weapon," Marnie murmured.

Cara flashed her a warning glare.

Bean struck a dramatic pose. "To the bonfire! Where secrets are s'mored and friendships are roasted back to life!"

They all broke out in peals of laughter, and began to gather their supplies with fresh energy.

CHAPTER 3

beach brawl

A maniacal cackle from outside their bonfire circle pierced the night. Eyes wide, Cara spun her head, searching for the culprit that shattered their peace.

"You've got to be kidding me!" Marnie's voice sliced through the dusk like a rotary cutter through a rogue seam allowance.

Cara had dropped her marshmallow stick. Marnie jabbed her stick into the flames a little too forcefully. "I swear, if I see his face, I'm going to use this." She twisted the stick into a blazing log.

That was harsh, even for Marnie. Cara bristled. *Darryl certainly has a talent for showing up at the exact moment no one wants him. Which is technically—every moment.*

"What now?" Haze asked from her driftwood seat, already setting her lemonade down with a sigh.

Bean, sitting close by, shrugged. The beach had been peaceful for about five minutes, which was about how long it took for Cara to almost believe they'd managed to shake off the earlier strain. The flickering bonfire, the sticky-sweet smell of marshmallows, the gentle rhythm of the ocean—it had all lulled her into a false sense of retreat.

"Well, well, what do we have here? A bunch of old ladies pretending to enjoy themselves?"

Darryl! A ghastly man with better timing and worse manners.

In the light of the fire, he flashed a grin that made Cara's teeth clench. He had sauntered up with an easy gait, his hands stuffed into the pockets of his battered jacket, his eyes gleaming with malice. "Heard you were out here having a party. Figured you could use some entertainment."

Haze muttered something under her breath.

"What?" Cara asked.

"Nothing." Haze's shoulders were stiff. She reached for her lemonade with a clenched jaw. "Let's just say I've had enough of Darryl's *business proposals* to last me a lifetime."

Cara raised an eyebrow. "Business proposals?"

"Doesn't matter." Haze's voice was flat. "He knows I said no. He just doesn't like being told that."

Cara didn't push.

Marnie stepped forward before Cara could stop her.

Here we go. She'll end up arrested for brawling on the beach before the night is out.

Her espresso-brown hair was windblown, and her jaw

was set tight. "Some nerve, coming back here again. You got a death wish?" Marnie growled.

"Oh, come on," Darryl drawled. "Don't get your pincushions in a twist."

Trudy's curls quivered as she whispered, "Don't engage, don't engage." She clutched her pastel mug of cocoa like it might be holy water.

Darryl shrugged, his grin widening. "I'm just enjoying the same beach as everyone else. But then again, I know things about everyone here . . . don't I, Bean?" His gaze shifted to Bean.

How does he know about our personal lives?

Bean's face hardened. "Shut up, Darryl."

"Oh, touchy, touchy," Darryl jeered. "I bet all your little quilting secrets wouldn't sound so cute if they got out. Some people might not be so understanding."

Haze had been quiet all evening, until Darryl showed up. His insinuation was enough to ignite every ember of resentment lingering from the day. The quilters were supposed to be a tight-knit group, but Darryl had a way of unraveling them. She fiddled with her earrings—the small metal charms clinking together like warning bells.

"Leave. Now," Cara said, stepping between Marnie and Darryl. Her voice didn't tremble, but her knees did.

Darryl tilted his head. "You're a little mouthy one, aren't you?"

Bean rose suddenly. Her glittery flip-flops squeaked in the sand as she stood, her red curls haloed in the firelight and her hands were clenched.

Cara exchanged a glance with Haze, who stood now also. Haze moved with a sigh. "This is foolish."

"You don't know anything about us," Marnie spat. She stepped forward so quickly her scarf fluttered behind her like a battle flag. "You're just a washed-up, no-good, beachcomber, who's angry at the world because you couldn't cut it. At anything." Her head bobbed with each insult, and spittle flew from her mouth with the last words.

The fire popped loudly, punctuating the heavy mood around them. Darryl's smile faltered for a moment, but then it returned, more vicious than before. "You think you're so much better, Marnie? You, with your holier-than-thou attitude? Maybe you ought to look in the mirror."

They were surrounding him now—not with fists, but with fury. Even Trudy—wide-eyed and hugging herself—stood.

Her friends started to circle around the man. Almost like a mob. But there was something primal in the way they inched forward—their collective presence a force for him to back down and go away.

"Darryl, leave us alone!" Trudy cried out, her smile gone.

"Or what?" Darryl jeered back at them. "What're you going to do, hit me with a quilt?"

"Let's not fight," Bean chirped, her voice almost as high as Trudy's. "Maybe we can just roast marshmallows together?"

"He can roast in hell," Marnie shoved him backward.

The moment unfolded like badly pieced quilt seams—disjointed, chaotic, and unraveling fast.

"Hey! Watch it, Grandma Hulk!"

Marnie advanced again, they were dangerously close to the fire, but Darryl stood his ground this time.

"You crazy witch!" he bellowed, shoving back.

"Witch. Me? Sure, I'll put a hex on you!"

More like a hexagon! Cara chuckled, even in the face of the threat.

"Grandma this!" Marnie yelled, plucking her burning hot marshmallow skewer out of the fire and swinging it like a saber.

Whoa, noooo! "Stop," Cara yelled as Darryl jumped backward out of Marnie's swing. "He's not worth it!" She rushed around to Marnie's side, attempting to intervene.

"You want to spend the night explaining this to the police? Because I guarantee *he* will," Haze interrupted, pointing at the man.

"Oh, I'll do more than that," Darryl barked. "I'll press charges. I'll tell everyone what really happened last fall. How about that, Bean? Want to talk about your little 'incident'?"

Bean froze. Her body stiffened like a starched quilt block.

Cara glanced between them all—her friends, tangled in rage and fear, with Darryl at the center of it. But he was more than a pest. He was a lit match in a room full of kindling.

Suddenly, a passerby intervened. "Hey! Hey, break it up!" His voice boomed over the crackling fire.

Everyone turned. A barrel-chested man in a pineapple-print shirt marched toward them, the little dog he was walking, yipping at his side.

The stranger pushed between Darryl and the quilters, his dog now barking wildly at the commotion. "What's going on here?"

Marnie stepped back. Darryl, rubbing his shoulder where Marnie had pushed him, grimaced and stepped away also.

"Are you people trying to reenact WrestleMania?" the man asked. "If you are, you better cool it. Or I'm calling the cops. Meatball and I don't approve of violence." The dog yipped once more.

Bean whispered, "The dog's name is Meatball?"

"Bean!" Cara hissed.

Darryl spat. "The whole lot of you have sand for brains. You'll regret this. Mark my words. You haven't seen the last of me." He jabbed a finger toward Bean. "Especially you." Then he vanished into the dark.

"That was a threat! You heard it," Cara said to the dog walker, gesturing toward the space Darryl had previously occupied.

The stranger gave a wary glance in the same direction, then his gaze dropped down to his dog. "Yep. Heard it. But I've also heard enough." He tugged lightly on the leash. "Come on, Meatball. Let's go sniff something less volatile."

The little dog gave a final yap, jumped around kicking up sand, and then trotted off after his human.

Marnie sank onto a log. Her dramatic lipstick was smudged. Her chest heaved with adrenaline and—maybe—fear.

"Well. That . . . happened," Trudy said, blinking too fast. "Does anyone want a s'mores?"

"We're done here," Haze said. She kicked sand over the edge of the fire pit and then walked back to the cottage. No one said a word as they followed.

The moment they stepped through the door, they dispersed like bobbins knocked off a sewing table. A gust rattled the framed screen of the cottage's back door. Cara sat frozen on the edge of her bed, the Storm at Sea quilt wrapped tight around her shoulders. She stared out into the dark and a floorboard creaked in the hallway.

Darryl was unhinged. But he'd also known too much. And tomorrow, he'd still be out there. Plotting.

As she lay in bed, a knot grew in her stomach. *Will I ever get to sleep tonight?*

CHAPTER 4

Snipped

The next morning, the air carried an eerie stillness on the beach, as if the ocean itself knew something was amiss. Cara put on a brave face, fumbling with her earrings, a nervous habit from her days working in traveling sales—*whoever said it would be fun selling fabric to quilt shops lied to me.* Anxiety was bubbling up in her chest again. The weight of the previous night hung over her tight group of friends like a storm cloud that refused to dissipate.

"All right, ladies," she said, forcing a cheerful tone as they set up their beachside quilts and snacks. "Let's not let last night ruin our day. How about we focus on enjoying the sunshine and sea breeze?"

Marnie flashed a thin and tired smile, barely masking the exhaustion etched beneath her eyes. Bean was silent, and the others busied themselves unpacking, when a scream pierced the air.

Everyone's heads snapped toward the shriek. A beach goer—with wide, terrified eyes—came hustling from the direction of the dunes, waving frantically.

"Help! Someone call the police!" the woman in a floppy hat shouted as she stumbled to their group. "There's a man . . . a body! Come."

Marnie's warm face had gone pale and Haze was already on her feet. They all followed the woman back toward the dunes. Cara's sandals slipped in the soft sand, and Bean clutched the brim of her sunhat during the grim march. Trudy muttered prayers under her breath, words half-lost to the ocean.

The shaken woman led them around a rise of tall grass, her gestures jerky and desperate. Cara's fingers found her spool-shaped earring, rubbing the familiar ridges as if the little charm could anchor her to steadiness.

At the dunes, Cara's worst fears had materialized. A lifeless figure lay crumpled on the beach, half-covered in sand, and face down. *Darryl Cunningham.* His skin was ashen, and a gash on his head had seeped blood onto the sand.

Bean made a noise like a squeaky toy deflating. "Maybe he's just . . . sound asleep?"

"Oh no!" Cara whispered, backing away, her heart pounding.

The floppy hat lady yelled at them. "Why are you all standing here? Will you please call 9-1-1!"

Bean crossed her arms. With trembling hands, Cara fumbled for her phone and dialed the emergency number.

"I'm calling," she stammered, pressing the phone to her ear.

"Nine-one-one, what's your emergency?" came the operator's calm voice.

"There's a man . . . He's not breathing," Cara blurted, glancing nervously at the woman, who was pacing back and forth, kneading her floppy hat and kicking up tufts of sand all around the crime scene. "We're at the beach, by the ocean. He looks . . . dead!"

"Stay calm, ma'am. Can you tell me your exact location?" the operator prompted, her tone steady and reassuring.

"Yes! We're near the boardwalk, by the sand dunes. Just off the main path!" Cara's voice trembled, the urgency of the situation creeping into her words. "Please hurry!"

"Help is on the way. Can you tell me how you found him?"

Cara glanced back at the group, who were all hovering around, their expressions ranging from shock to fear. "It was a beach goer who found him. I don't know how long he's been here!"

"Okay, stay with me, ma'am. Help is coming. I need you to remain on the line until they arrive. Can you do that?"

"Yes."

Dread crept into Cara's bones. *I'm the one who insisted we come here. I wanted peace. Instead, I signed us up to be murder suspects.* Bile rose up in her throat. *What have we* stumbled into? First, he acts like a pompous turd; now he washes up dead!

TIME STRETCHED OUT FOREVER, but it was really mere minutes until the beach was swarming with police cordoning off the area with yellow tape.

And by the time the paramedics left, the beach had turned from an idyllic retreat to an active crime scene.

A uniformed officer, his notebook in hand, approached the quilters as they stood, grouped together a distance away. "Ladies, I'm going to need to ask you some questions."

Due to the public brawl the night before, they were likely the last people seen with Darryl. *And in a heated confrontation. I knew this was going to go bad.*

One by one, they were pressed to give their statements.

Marnie went first, standing tall and rigid, her tone clipped and defensive.

Bean fidgeted with the hem of her shirt, eyes darting like a guilty sparrow, glancing toward the dunes as if hoping the waves might wash the whole mess away.

Trudy absentmindedly offered the officer a cookie, her hand hovering mid-air in awkward hospitality.

Haze adjusted the waistband of her linen pants, delivering her account like a witness giving a presentation—every word calculated and intentional.

Cara had hoped that by the time it was her turn, her

nerves would have settled. But as the officer asked her questions, her pulse quickened.

The officer flipped through his notes with a raised brow and a smug look. "I understand there was an altercation with the deceased last night. Can you tell me what happened?"

She swallowed hard. "Yes, there was . . . a disagreement. Darryl was antagonizing us—insulting the women, making threats. It got heated, and there may have been some pushing, but nothing more. Not one of the quilters would hurt him."

The officer scribbled in his notebook. "This is just about you right now, ma'am. Can anyone confirm your whereabouts after the altercation?"

"We all went back to the rental house. Together."

The officer's attention remained fixed, but Cara sensed his scrutiny. To her surprise, he simply thanked her curtly and moved on.

Trudy chewed on the tip of her sunglasses, no doubt scheming a way to put a positive spin on the situation. *Is it too early to be happy that at least he won't bother us anymore?* Cara's fingers reached for her earring.

Each of them had a motive for wanting him silenced, even if hers was thin. The argument last night wasn't the first time Darryl had caused trouble for any of them, and the secrets he'd hinted at . . . *I need to find out what was going on between Darryl and the other women. How much could they really have wanted to keep him quiet?*

A police car pulled up and a man in a gray blazer

stepped out, his hair in wild disarray and his shoes sinking awkwardly into the sand. *Detective Thistlewitt.* She was aware of his reputation from locals—a legend in his own mind. Quirky, meticulous, and with a knack for getting into the thick of things quickly.

He approached the quilters and the scene, his eyes darting over the group, taking them in with a discerning glance. "Detective Reggie Thistlewitt," he said, his voice upbeat in contrast to the somber mood, his hand outstretched. "Looks like we've got a bit of a puzzle here, ladies, and I'm left wondering how five quilters fit into it."

Cara shook his hand and sputtered her name. The quirk of his eyebrow suggested he was serious about the investigation. And the way he said "puzzle" made her uneasy. "We're just bystanders. I assure you."

"Mm-hmm. Well, if it's all the same with you, you're not to leave town just yet." There was no humor in his eyes. The women murmured acceptance, and he continued, "I do have some questions, and I think we'll be seeing a lot of each other over the next few days."

Yup, we're suspects. All of us.

Detective Thistlewitt quickly moved on to speak with the officer in charge.

"We need to talk," Bean said, her voice tight with urgency.

Marnie nodded. "Not here." Her gaze darted to the detective and officer and back to Bean.

"What are we going to do? We didn't do anything!" Haze said, her voice wavering. "Right?"

Cara's stomach churned. She wanted to say something reassuring, but her mind was racing with doubt. The problem wasn't whether she had done it—it was that she couldn't be sure about the others. There were cracks between them—little tensions, unspoken rifts, secrets teased but never shared. *What if one of those cracks has split wide open? Darryl said he knew our secrets? Secrets I don't even know—maybe big enough to push one of them too far?*

"We stick together," Cara said, reaching out her arm for Bean—who was standing next to her—though her voice was hollow. "We didn't do anything wrong. So, we'll try to figure out who did it before they try to pin it on one of us."

They had no choice now. They had to investigate for their own sakes.

Thistlewitt watched them from where he stood with the other officer, and Cara couldn't tell if he was curious or certain.

Either way, the clock is ticking now. One of them might already be lying . . . Or next.

CHAPTER 5

Secrets

Cara had expected their days to be filled with laughter and the comforting hum of sewing machines, not clouded by death or suspicions of causing it. The five women gathered in the airy, white-washed living room of their rented cottage—once a beachside family home, now filled with the scent of starch. Their fabric and supplies spread out over the tables and furniture, the mood was anything but lighthearted. Cara glanced around the room at her friends, each hunched over projects they barely touched, moving their needles with muscle memory more than focus. The fan overhead clacked with each slow rotation, stirring humid air.

Sitting at the table closest to Cara, with her brown hair twisted up extra tightly, Marnie wrinkled her bright red lips while stabbing a needle through a batik star block, like it owed her money. Her quilt bag, filled with hoarded scraps, spilled onto the floor beside her chair.

Bean hummed—off-key and oblivious—as she arranged tiny fussy-cut flip-flops into the corner of her beach appliqué scene, her frizzy red curls spilling from a sun hat she refused to take off indoors. Her bright pink novelty T-shirt read: *Sewciopath*.

That's comforting. Cara resisted a chuckle.

Tucked into the corner, sitting in a cute sewing chair upholstered in a multi-colored thimble print, Haze was ruthlessly chain-piecing—not a stray thread on her perfectly pressed linen capris. She flipped open her notebook of carefully labeled fabric swatches.

And Trudy, smiling way too brightly, was "working" on a log cabin block that hadn't changed much in an hour —her fingers fussed with fabrics over and over while her eyes darted toward the window. The monogrammed tote at her feet was still fully zipped.

Cara set down her piecing and cleared her throat. Determined to exonerate her friends' names and uncover the truth about Darryl's death, she forced her voice to steady.

"Marnie, can I ask you something?" Cara finger-pressed the seam of a flying-geese block flat with extra care. "Is there anything you've been keeping from us? I mean, about Darryl or . . . well, anything we should know?"

The "sassmaster" didn't answer right away. Marnie jabbed her needle into the project, yanked it tight, then glanced up, her brow arching in that dramatic way she did when caught off guard.

"Me? No, of course not!" Her laugh broke. "I'm just

busy with these scraps." She motioned her hand toward the chaotic pile of half-folded fabric next to her, where bold jewel tones clashed like a family reunion brawl.

"Really? I don't mean just this minute. It's just—I've been feeling like everyone here is carrying something."

"Okay, fine. I'm a bit tight on cash right now," Marnie replied. "Some unexpected bills, a few too many online fabric orders, and a credit card I've been avoiding. I didn't want to drag anyone into it. So, yes, I'm carrying that. But it's not about Darryl! I swear."

I don't think she has any motive, but she did shove him at the beach. Cara nodded slowly. "That sounds like every quilter I know," she said with a sympathetic snort. "Thank you for sharing that."

Marnie's mouth twitched into a reluctant smile. She dropped her voice conspiratorially. "Don't tell Haze this, but I may have tried to use a quilting coupon to buy dog treats last week."

Zipping her lips, Cara smiled, then said, "Your secret's safe with me."

Filled with the muted snips of scissors and the puffs of steam from the iron, the atmosphere relaxed for a moment.

The afternoon sun filtered in hazy gold, casting a spotlight on Trudy's untouched blocks.

Cara's gaze landed next on Bean, who was hunched over her beach quilt with the intensity of a kid frosting a gingerbread house.

"Bean," Cara said, gently scooting closer to her friend. "You haven't said much today. Are *you* okay?"

Bean blinked. "Oh, *I'm* fine! Just trying to decide if this tiny umbrella should go above the flamingo or the sandcastle." She held up the appliqué piece.

Cara managed a tired grin. "Classic Bean." But she pressed on. "Bean, what's your history with Darryl? I can't shake the feeling there's more to this whole thing," Cara asked, gauging the fiery red-head's reaction.

The playful spark in Bean's expression dimmed. She dropped the umbrella onto the table. "He was a bully, plain and simple. I had a run-in with him a few years back when he accused me of ruining his sandcastle on the beach. It was absolutely ridiculous, and trivial. I told him I had nothing to do with it, but he never believed me," she admitted, her tone flat but heavy with disdain.

"Did it escalate beyond that?" Darryl getting into a physical altercation with any woman, let alone her best friends made her sick.

Bean glanced away, her jaw tightening. "Let's just say our paths have crossed more than once, and it's never been pleasant."

Does Bean have a motive? Nothing was ever *pleasant with that guy.*

Cara hesitated. Her hands moved—but her mind had drifted backward.

I remember when the only drama in the group was whether to use navy or teal in the charity quilts for their guild.

Two years ago, a surprise storm had rolled in during their retreat, canceling all of their outdoor plans. With the power flickering and rain pelting the windows like angry pebbles, they had dragged every battery-powered sewing light into the great room and declared a "Frankenquilt" challenge—one quilt, five opinions, no rules.

Marnie had insisted on using her bold jewel tones, while Haze lobbied for a cohesive minimalist palette. Trudy kept sneaking in novelty prints when no one was looking—tiny cats and flamingos that made Bean cackle like a kid on Halloween.

They'd laughed so hard that weekend her stomach hurt for days after. Even when the power went out completely and they were left to hand-quilt by flashlight, the mood had been light, silly, and safe. They'd joked about entering the Frankenquilt into the state fair under the name "Group Therapy."

Now, Cara barely got a full sentence out of them without worry lacing the edges. They were all here in the same room again, surrounded by thread and fabric, but the stitching between them was coming undone.

She wanted—needed—to believe in them. These were her people. They had always shared retreats, room keys, scraps, late-night confessions over wine and bobbins. But now, doubt crept in.

Back in the present, Cara stepped up to the ironing board and pressed the iron down a little too hard on a flying-geese unit and whispered a quiet apology to the block.

Bean had returned to her appliqué, humming softly under her breath like the past five minutes hadn't happened at all.

Cara gave her a tired smile, then shifted her focus across the room.

Haze and Trudy were engaged in their own debate over which half-square triangle method was the best—nine at once from a square or using paper foundation sheets.

Waiting for them to finish, Cara queried, "Haze, can I ask you something?"

Hazel, lovingly nicknamed Haze by her friends, stopped stitching and peered up at Cara with a friendly smile. "Sure. What's on your mind?"

Cara hesitated, weighing her words. "I know things got a little heated with Darryl, but was there something else between you and him that you'd want to tell us?"

Haze checked a calculation on her quilting watch and scratched something on a sticky note, the smile fading as she glanced at Trudy. *Is Haze ignoring me? Or just thinking.*

With her tongue out and one eye squinted shut, Trudy was hunched over her block, quietly trying to thread her needle. She missed again and huffed.

Cara chortled. "If you can't thread the needle, then needle the thread. Works every time."

"I swear that it's slippery," Trudy muttered. "Attitude!" She leaned closer, licked the end of the thread and tried again. Then, she popped up out of her seat with a victorious squeak—only to jab the needle into her cardigan cuff instead of her fabric. "Well, shoot. That was *almost* majestic."

Bean snorted. "Majestic adjacent."

Trudy gave a mock bow. "You're welcome for the entertainment, ladies. Just know if we ever *do* murder someone, I'll be the *distraction.*"

"Well, there was that time he tried to muscle in on my business," Haze admitted, her voice low. "He wanted to buy my fabric line for some beach-themed idea."

Haze's lips thinned. "He cornered me during intermission at the Mystic guild show—my arms full of fat quarters, my machine already packed, and there was nowhere to escape."

She stared at her swatch notebook. "He held up one of my tide-line prints like it was a garage-sale flyer. Said, '*Your fabric, my charm—beach tourists would eat it up.*'" Her voice had dropped into a passable impression of Darryl's faux-suave pitch.

"He actually said that? Gross."

"Yeah. Went on about opening a beachfront shop, the foot traffic, how all we needed was 'a handshake and a little flexibility.'" Haze snorted. "I told him I sell art, not souvenirs."

The tiniest crack formed in the tone of her voice. "That's when his tone changed. And he got really weird. Said, '*Everyone's selling something. The only question is who gets paid.*' Like I owed him for saying no or something?"

She flipped a page with more force than needed. "He wanted exclusive rights. Told me I'd be smart to let a man 'handle the marketing.' When I refused, he started lurking at local shows—always nearby when I spoke to buyers. Never did anything that could be pinned down, just was there enough to make me look . . . shady too."

Unease crawled across her skin. "He really tried to tank your business?"

"In public he was all smiles and aloha shirts. In private?" Haze peered up, voice flat. "He was a vulture in flip-flops." She flipped another page. "I declined, of course, and he didn't take it well."

A hundred tiny alarms went off in Cara's brain. *It seems like Haze has the biggest motive at this point.*

"Haze, that's not nothing," Cara said, lowering her voice. "He wasn't exactly the quilting type."

Trudy harrumphed from across the room, tugging at a thread stuck to her sleeve. "He wasn't."

"So, what *was* he actually after?" Cara glanced between Haze and Trudy.

Haze laughed, dry, low and uncharacteristically bitter. "Oh, believe me, I saw through him right away. It wasn't just about the fabric."

"What do you mean?" Cara tilted her head, more intrigued.

"It became a sob story about starting a beachside boutique—selling 'authentic, handmade' goods to tourists. Said he needed local artists to supply him. I thought, maybe he just wanted to make a buck off my designs. But the more he talked, the clearer it got—he didn't give a dang about my fabric or any handmade boutique."

Cara contemplated the conversation, finishing her geese blocks. She pulled the piecing out from under the pressor foot and cut her thread.

Haze scowled, glancing again at Trudy. "He made some pretty nasty comments afterward, much like the crapola he spewed here already. Said I'd regret turning him away, that my designs would never sell without his influence, etcetera."

Haze grimaced. "He started spreading rumors. Said my last workshop had been a disaster—that I copied other designers. Nothing stuck—but it made me appear unstable, petty. That was his thing. Whisper and watch people unravel."

"Did he threaten you?" Trudy asked.

"No, not outright," Haze replied. "But for a while, I kept seeing him everywhere. It felt like he was always lurking around, waiting for a chance to strike at me—like the snake he is."

Trudy had shifted in her seat and gone quiet.

"Did he try the same pitch on you, Trudy?" Cara asked.

"Yeah." Trudy didn't peer up. "He came to me, too. Same boutique story. Told me he could help get me out of the teaching circuit—that I could finally sell something with my name on it, not just someone else's pattern."

Cara stilled. "You said that deal was nothing. Just talk."

Trudy met her eyes. "It started that way. Then the table turned. Said he had documents he could twist to make it seem like I'd used guild retreat funds for a personal gain."

Haze's mouth tightened. "He was such a scumbag!"

"Said things like, '*You'd be amazed how quickly people believe what they want to hear.*'"

A slow throb of anger built up behind Cara's eyes.

"I didn't kill him," Trudy blurted, twisting a bobbin between her fingers. "But I panicked. As soon as he showed up dead, I deleted everything. I didn't want anyone to know I'd been involved with him at all. She swallowed hard, eyes darting to the floor. "I didn't even know if he just... fell and hit his head, or if something darker had happened. I wasn't taking any chances."

"You should've told us," Haze said flatly, her arms folding tight across her chest.

"I know." She returned to her bobbin unspooling the thread from it.

Cara's throat tightened. "Who knows what else he was doing." *I should be relieved I never had any run-ins with him. But am I? Or was I just next in line to learn how ugly he could really be?*

She glanced from one woman to the next, trying to imagine them being cornered by Darryl, and if one could've broken down until they thought hiding was safer than telling the truth. "Thank you for sharing that, Trudy. We all need to be clear about what's really at stake if the police determine his death wasn't an accident."

The bobbin rolled from Trudy's lap and hit the floor with a *plink*.

Haze sighed, her shoulders easing slightly. "I just wish we could forget about him and focus on our quilting."

"Well," Trudy added quickly, standing with sudden purpose. "Since we're on the topic of things no one likes—how about I go warm up that cinnamon coffee cake I brought?" She didn't wait for a response, already bustling toward the kitchen.

Marnie rolled her eyes. "That's a deflective response if I've ever heard one."

But Cara didn't smile. *Trudy is lying. Not well, but she is.* She stood to stretch her back, eyes drifting toward the kitchen area where Trudy had just escaped the conversation in a cloud of cheer and avoidance.

"I'll go help her," Cara offered, already on her feet.

Rummaging in the fridge, Trudy's back was to the living room. The air smelled faintly of cinnamon, and lemon dish soap.

"You okay?" Cara asked gently.

Trudy yelped as one hand flew to her chest. "Jeez, you startled me."

"Sorry."

She grabbed the foil-covered cake, then hip-checked the refrigerator door shut. "I'm fine, just grabbing the coffee cake. Totally normal snack time behavior. Nothing weird here," Trudy chirped.

Cara leaned casually against the island while the other three conversed over purring sewing machines, oblivious to Cara and Trudy. "You know, if there's anything else you want to talk about, Trudy . . ."

"Nope! Sugar and carbs will do the trick."

As she turned toward the microwave, a small folded slip fell from the pocket of her cardigan. It fluttered to the floor near Cara's feet.

Trudy didn't seem to notice so Cara stooped to pick it up, eyes flicking over the header before she could stop herself.

Coastal Bank - Check
Visible beneath the fold:
Bank Check: $2,500
Pay to: D. Cunningham

SHE STOOD SLOWLY, pressing the receipt into Trudy's hand as casually as she could. "You dropped this."

Trudy blinked, then smiled casually. "Thanks. Old grocery list."

She stuffed it into her pocket without another word.

Cara didn't press. *Not yet, but now she's at the top of my suspect list.*

But as Trudy sliced the cake and launched into a bubbly monologue about cinnamon being a natural mood booster, Cara's mind spun faster than a bobbin winder at full speed.

Why would Trudy pay Darryl any money, never mind that sum—and what was she trying to buy from him?

"Okay, let's have cake," Bean said, turning in her chair toward her friends in the kitchen.

A sharp knock echoed throughout the beach house.

Trudy froze mid-slice, the serrated knife suspended above the cinnamon coffee cake.

Bean fumbled her snips and they hit the wooden floor with a metallic clattering *ting*.

Marnie stood abruptly. She muttered a curse under her breath, eyes narrowing toward the front door.

Then came a second knock—slower this time, but heavier, and more deliberate.

Cara's mind scrambled through the possibilities. *Is it Detective Thistlewitt returning with more questions? What will everyone say? And more urgently—what won't they say? What'll happen to Trudy?*

Maybe it's another officer, come to take one of us in? Or —worse—?

The third knock landed like punctuation. Just one, firm, almost final rap, and the silence that followed was somehow louder than the knock itself.

CHAPTER 6

unraveling seams

An electrical charge filled the air, like the moment before a storm cracks through the sky. Marnie squared her shoulders and reached for the doorlock. When the door creaked open, Detective Thistlewitt stood there, clipboard in hand, and Cara exhaled audibly. Marnie stepped aside and he entered.

"Good afternoon, ladies," he said, his voice crisp. "I appreciate your cooperation as I continue my investigation into Mr. Cunningham's unfortunate demise."

"Of course," Cara motioned for him to take a seat, clearing a pile of fabric away to make space for him on the couch. "We're here to help."

"Let's get started then, shall we?" Detective Thistlewitt leaned forward, the corner of his eyes wrinkling. "I need to clarify your alibis from last night. Where, specifically, were each of you during the time of the murder?"

So he was murdered, well that solves that question.

The other quilters exchanged nervous glances.

"When exactly was he killed?" Cara asked Thistlewitt.

"Too early to say for sure, but we estimate between midnight and sunrise."

That's not very precise. Is he being vague on purpose?

Marnie rolled the edge of her sleeve between her fingers. "I was in my room," she said without being asked directly. "Working on my quilt. I didn't leave until the morning."

We all were, weren't we? Cara began to wonder.

Bean's head bobbed. "Me too! I was finishing my project in my room also." She smoothed her hands over her knees, then added quickly, "I was up for a bit, but then I crashed."

Detective Thistlewitt didn't look up from his notepad. "What time?"

Bean hesitated, chewing on her lip. "Um... before midnight. Definitely before midnight."

"Same here," Trudy added, her voice shaky. "I was really tired from the beach."

Nodding, Haze said, "Me too."

Cara's heart panged. She wanted to believe them all. She really did. Any one of them could have left the house without her or anyone else knowing. *Could they all possibly be in on it together?* When the eyes all turned to her suddenly, she added her own vague account of an early night. *All the same alibi, everyone went to bed and no one left the house. Thistlewitt must be mistaken. It's impossible that it could be one of her friends.*

The detective leaned back, folding his arms as if waiting for a punchline, a skeptical eyebrow raised. "Interesting. So, none of you left the house after returning from the bonfire?"

"No," they chorused. As the detective volleyed another pointed question their way, Cara's attention was laser-focused on her friends. Marnie and Bean had sat back down. Even Haze, who could usually sew through a hurricane, had gone perfectly still—her fingers resting on a stack of neatly trimmed half-square triangles. If Cara didn't know better, she'd have thought they were all trying not to act guilty. Which would've been fine—except it made them all look guilty.

Her stomach twisted. *Is this what it looks like when someone in your group is hiding something? Or has committed a crime? Or is it just natural for law abiding citizens when confronted by a detective. I don't know.* She warred with herself, never having been in this type of situation before.

Scanning the room—not looking for anything in particular—Cara just needed to look somewhere other than at Detective Thistlewitt's narrowed eyes and suspicious glare. Her eyes drifted over their scattered fabric piles, hoping to ground herself in the disarray of quilting supplies. But something metallic winked at her from the floor. Cara shifted and leaned forward, squinting. A small silver curve peeked out from beneath the overstuffed chair. She reached over and pinched it between her fingers. A bracelet charm. *Marnie's. That's strange.*

She turned it over in her hand, the chonky sewing machine charm etched with a bejeweled *M*. Cara lifted it slowly. "Marnie, is this yours?"

Marnie's eyes flicked to the bracelet, then to Cara, then back again. Her posture stiffened like she'd been caught mid-lie in a game of Two Truths and a Lie. "Uh, yeah!" The woman reached out her hand for it. "Thanks, I must've dropped it earlier." But her voice wavered at the end.

Marnie's hand went to her throat, like she wasn't sure where her necklace was either, though a sterling silver pendant drop hung perfectly at her collarbone.

"You said you didn't leave," Cara said slowly, softly.

Marnie's lips parted, then pressed into a tight line. "It —it must've fallen off when I was working on my quilt earlier," she said, her tone climbing a half-step too high. "I was so focused on my project." Her voice wavered and she rubbed her palms together.

Trudy cleared her throat, loud and theatrical.

For one sickening beat, Cara let a notion form in her thoughts. *If someone here killed him, could I blame them?*

Darryl had been a vile, manipulating menace. The idea that someone might've snapped on him didn't seem far-fetched. But the thought turned bitter on her tongue. *Each has a similar motive, and equal opportunity to have snuck out of the house when everyone else was sleeping. But* that *seems less like a 'wits end situation' and more like premeditation. That couldn't be one of my friends.*

She lowered the bracelet gently into Marnie's hand. "I

just thought it was strange. That's all," she said steadily. "Didn't want it to get lost."

Detective Thistlewitt harrumphed, and his eyes flickered between them. "It's essential to be truthful, especially in times like these. Any inconsistencies in your stories could lead to serious implications for the *entire* group."

Doubt settled into Cara's mind again like a heavy fog. Ever since Darryl's death, everything felt like a clue. *A bracelet under the furniture shouldn't matter. But does it in this context.* "Marnie, are you sure you didn't see Darryl after the bonfire?" she asked gently, hoping to coax the truth out of her friend.

"I didn't! I told you!" Marnie snapped, crossing her arms defiantly.

"Okay, okay," Cara replied, her hands becoming clammy.

"I'll need to speak to each of you," Thistlewitt barked.

As the detective pulled out his notepad, an overwhelming urge to defend her friends surge through Cara, but what if one of them was hiding something more sinister than just losing a bracelet?

"Alibis don't mean much ladies, when everyone in the house shares one," he said, his tone deceptively light. "Especially when the victim had dirt on all of you."

Before Cara could process her emotions further, a loud crash came from the kitchen, followed by a clatter.

The quilters exchanged wide-eyed glances. "What was that?" Bean exclaimed.

Cara darted across the living room, skirting around a

pile of fat quarters and the ironing board teetering on uneven flooring. The detective's knock had already rattled her, but the crash from the kitchen sent her nerves into full retreat. "I'll check it out," she said on her way, not looking back.

The open layout gave her a full view into the kitchen even before her bare feet crossed to the tile. And she stopped cold.

A squirrel—enormous by squirrel standards, a puffed-up gray monstrosity with beady black eyes and a tail like a feather duster gone rogue—stood frozen on the center of the butcher block island. Around its paws lay the remains of a plastic cutlery basket, now overturned, with spoons and forks strewn like party confetti across the floor.

A beat passed and Cara blinked, thinking it was a mirage.

The squirrel blinked back. Then its tiny chest heaved and its bushy tail twitched. And in the strange, suspended moment, Cara swore she saw regret in its eyes. Maybe even shame. Or more likely it was pure, unfiltered panic.

Then it bolted. Or tried to, its claws clicking frantically as it struggled for traction.

First, it skittered across the countertop, knocking over a half-empty bag of flour and leaving a ghostly cloud in its wake. Next came a stool—used as a springboard—then a leap that would've made an Olympic gymnast proud. It landed briefly on the ironing board, sending a stack of charm squares tumbling to the floor, before launching again.

With the grace of a caffeinated ninja, the squirrel jetted itself across the rest of the kitchen, tail flicking, and disappeared through the small doggy door cut out of the back door—leaving nothing but disarray and the fading sound of the flapping vinyl door behind it.

Cara stared at the empty space where it had been. "What in the—?"

Behind her, footsteps thudded across the tiles as Bean skidded into view, eyes wide. "Was that a flying hamster?"

Trudy appeared next, hand still clutching a mug. "Did something explode?"

Haze followed at a slower pace, arms crossed, gaze sharp. "Please tell me that squirrel didn't touch my binding strips."

Cara, half-laughing, half-horrified, turned toward the others. "No fatalities. Unless you count the flour. Or Marnie's stack of charm squares."

From the living area, Marnie groaned. "Those were sorted by color!" She stood and walked over to Cara.

"Well," Cara brushed a spoon away with her foot. "Looks like someone else cracked under questioning."

"We're gonna need more coffee for a day like today."

As they stood in the aftermath, the group burst into laughter—snorting and giggling. Just for a moment, the murder, secrets, and all suspicious glances—vanished behind rodent-induced hysteria.

Detective Thistlewitt stood in the doorway, frowning, hand poised above the buckle holstering his weapon, observing them. He shook his head. "It seems even a detective's inquiry can't compete with the antics of rogue wildlife," he said, a small smile breaking through his pursed lips.

The group's laughter still echoed faintly in the kitchen, but the high had already begun to wane. Bean was still giggling softly, dabbing her eyes with the hem of her T-shirt. Marnie leaned against the counter, cheeks pink from laughter—or maybe from relief.

But Cara couldn't shake it. That flicker in Marnie's eyes right before the squirrel stole the show, that tightness wasn't quite fear—but wasn't far from it either.

"Guess we all needed that." Trudy said, brushing flour from the counter.

The tension hadn't left. It had only buried itself under flour and tiny paw prints.

Cara moved to the edge of the kitchen, eyes on the doggy door. "Let's hope that squirrel's the only thing surprising us today."

CHAPTER 7

the quilters turn

Detective Thistlewitt had continued asking the same questions in slightly different ways, testing for weak seams in their stories. His parting resolve, that everyone needed to remain in tow, lingered long after he left.

As evening descended, the overstuffed couch, and chairs in the rental house became a flimsy refuge from the heaviness hanging over their vacation.

Cara curled up with a warm mug of cocoa, the steam rising in delicate tendrils as the flickering light from the television bathed the room in a soft glow. A romantic movie played on the screen, but the quilters barely paid attention, their thoughts obviously elsewhere. Cara's were tangled in the web of suspicion and doubt that had begun to fully ensnare her friends.

The flicker of light danced across Bean's face, half-shadowed and unreadable. They used to spend nights like this laughing until their sides ached.

"What was that line again?" Marnie asked, her voice too high-pitched, an anxious laugh escaping her lips in a failed attempt to lighten the mood. "Something about 'love conquering all'?"

"More like love *complicating* everything," Bean retorted, her brow furrowed as she focused on the screen, her lips pursed.

The atmosphere thickened as unspoken discord simmered just beneath the surface. It wasn't long before a spiraling conversation began.

"Honestly, how could you have forgotten to lock the door last night?" Marnie's voice raised, eyes narrowing at Bean. "You know Darryl could have walked right in!"

Bean shot back, "You think I'm the only one to blame? Think I'm an easy target because I'm kind. What about you?"

Cara shifted uncomfortably as her friends turned on each other. "Guys, please," she pleaded, attempting to defuse the situation. "This isn't helping anyone."

But her words fell on deaf ears. Marnie and Bean were in full swing now, hurling accusations like darts. And the tension in the room quickly reached a boiling point, and the camaraderie these two had once shared began to crumble, piece by piece.

"I can't believe you'd even think that," Marnie spat, her face flushed with anger. "You're the last person I would have expected this from, Bean."

"Maybe if you weren't so obsessed with keeping your financial troubles a secret, we wouldn't be in this mess!" Bean shot back, her voice shaking with fury.

Marnie's jaw dropped. "You think I'm the only one with secrets? Please. You cling to people's attention like it's oxygen. Darryl sniffed that out in two seconds."

Bean's eyes flashed with anger. "You're one to talk. You hoard fabric like it's gold bullion. Every retreat, your bags practically burst at the seams—and somehow you still need to 'borrow just one more fat quarter.'" She mimed air quotes with her fingers.

"That's not hoarding, that's being prepared," Marnie snapped. "Unlike you, who thinks being adorable and bubbly is a survival strategy."

"I don't try to be adorable!" Bean cried, her face flushing. "I'm just—being myself."

Haze set her scissors down with a sharp clack. "Enough. You're both being ridiculous. Whatever's going on, we're not going to figure it out by tearing each other to shreds."

"Oh, of course Haze thinks she's the voice of reason," Marnie said bitterly, arms crossed. "You'd probably hand out a spreadsheet to solve a murder."

"Better that than flying off the handle," Haze shot back.

"Guys," Trudy pleaded. "Please don't fight. We're all scared and tired."

Cara sat frozen on the couch, her mug cooling in her hands. She wanted to defend both of her friends. She wanted to believe none of this mattered. But she couldn't shake the question rising in her gut—*Did I miss the signs? Were the cracks in our friendships there all along, hidden beneath fabric and good intentions?*

"Maybe we don't know each other as well as we thought," she murmured.

The weight of the world, well at least the murder, hung on her shoulders, her loyalties torn between her two closest friends. "I don't want to choose sides!" she exclaimed, desperation creeping into her voice. "We need to stick together."

"Together?" Marnie parroted, throwing her hands up in frustration. "How can we when we can't even trust each other?"

The argument had escalated enough. It was time to stop the accusations. "Let's just take a break," Cara suggested, her heart heavy with the weight of their unraveling friendships. "We don't want to say things we can't take back."

With reluctant agreement, the quilters retreated to their corners of the room. Cara wrapped herself in a quilt, feeling the isolation wrap around her like a shroud.

Trudy sat rigidly in the armchair by the window, furiously ripping out a line of stitching with a seam ripper, the sharp little tool jerking with more force than necessary. Tiny threads floated to the braided carpet. She muttered to herself with each pull, but her words were too low for Cara to make out.

Haze stood by the ironing board, quietly refolding the

same stack of fat quarters for the third time. Her motions were precise—almost meditative—but her shoulders were tense. Every crease she pressed was a silent effort to flatten the emotional chaos in the room.

Marnie had disappeared to the back porch, the screen door clacking shut behind her. Cara made out the silhouette of her pacing, through the screen.

Cara pulled the quilt tighter around herself and closed her eyes briefly.

Maybe all of this isn't about Darryl, maybe it's all just about my friends?

Later, as the sound of the TV faded into the background, snippets of conversation drifted from the kitchen, their voices hushed.

Cara paused.

Haze's voice was low but firm. "I can't shake the feeling that Marnie knows more than she's letting on. It's not just her nervousness."

"I know," came the reply—Trudy's voice, unmistakable now. "You remember that day at the guild swap meet? Marnie left with Darryl. Said it was to pick up raffle prizes, but when she came back, she looked like she was struggling to not cry."

"She said it was allergies," Haze added. "But she doesn't even have allergies. She told me once she was practically immune to pollen."

Cara craned her neck, with her ear toward the conversation but it paused.

"She's hiding something," Trudy said. "I just don't know what."

And neither do I? Cara considered. *Is this just gossip, or is there any merit to it?*

THE MORNING LIGHT crept into Cara's room, casting a soft glow on her bedspread. She stirred, her sleep disturbed by the muffled sounds of the ocean and the faint rustling of someone else moving about. Groggy and bleary-eyed, she rolled over, glancing at the clock. *It's far too early for my liking, but my throat is parched.*

With a resigned sigh, she threw off the covers and padded down the hallway, the wooden floor cool beneath her feet. As she entered the kitchen, the smell of coffee wafted through the air, pulling her further from sleep.

To her surprise, she found Marnie standing at the counter, staring intently at her mug as if it held the answers to all their problems. The faint glow of the dawn illuminated her anxious expression.

"Marnie?" Cara called softly, rubbing the sleep from her eyes. "What are you doing up so early?"

Marnie jumped slightly, then turned to Cara, a look of urgency in her eyes. "Oh, Cara, I'm glad you're here. I had the strangest dream, and I think it might mean something."

"Really?" Cara raised an eyebrow, intrigued, despite her morning fatigue. "What was it about?"

"I dreamt that we were at the beach, but it wasn't just any beach," Marnie said, her voice low and conspiratorial. "There was something hidden in Darryl's beach shack—something so important I could almost see it!"

Cara's curiosity was piqued instantly. "Do you remember what it was?"

"No, but it felt urgent, like we needed to find it before someone else did," Marnie said, her eyes wide with conviction. "I know it sounds crazy, but what if there's something in there that can help us understand what happened?"

Excitement mixed with anxiety rushed through Cara's veins. "You want to go check it out? Right now?"

Marnie nodded, her determination evident. "We can't wait for the others. They're still sleeping, and who knows how long it'll take them to get moving. We need to act on this fast."

They exchanged glances, both feeling the weight of their predicament and the flicker of hope that perhaps this was the breakthrough they needed.

"Okay, let's get dressed quickly. If there's anything there, we should be the ones to find it."

The two women hurried to their rooms, Cara hastily throwing on clothes and grabbing her jacket. In a matter of minutes, they reconvened in the kitchen, whispering like schoolgirls on a secret mission.

"Do you think we should leave a note?" Cara asked with a flicker of doubt.

Marnie shook her head. "Nah. We won't be gone long.

Let's see if there's anything there first. We can decide what to do about it later."

With that, they slipped out of the house, tiptoeing, being careful not to wake the others. The early morning air was brisk as they made their way down the beach path.

As they approached Darryl's run-down beach shack, the salty breeze tangled in Cara's hair, and the unmistakable smell of mildew wrinkled her nose. *What secrets await us inside—and do I really want to find out?*

CHAPTER 8

loose threads

A chill of unease crept down Cara's spine.
She and Marnie scooted up the narrow path through the dunes, the wind whipping sand against their ankles like tiny, stinging warnings. Grasses hissed and bowed in the gusts, their dry stalks rattling against one another. The faint cries of gulls carried from in the distance, sounding less like playful beach chatter and more like mocking laughter.

With every step, Cara's mind staged its own protest. *Is this really a good idea?* They hadn't told the others where they were going. *What if someone is watching the shack right now?* The idea of being spotted—of drawing unwanted attention—sent a shiver through her. She glanced over her shoulder.

The smell of low tide grew stronger and mixed with the sour tang of mildew. Rotting seaweed had piled in a dark heap near the waterline. Marnie didn't seem to notice; she had her chin tucked down and her hands buried deep in her jacket pockets, her stride more determined than Cara's.

Cara slowed, eyeing multiple sets of footprints and an overturned, half-buried bucket in the sand.

"Someone's been here recently," she murmured. Whether it was the police, a curious beachcomber, or someone with darker motives, she didn't know—but her blood pressure rose all the same.

Darryl's beach shack slumped at the edge of the dunes like it had lost the will to stand straight. Weathered boards peeled with sun-bleached paint, and an uneven screen door hung from one hinge, creaking whenever the wind so much as breathed.

The roofline sagged under a collection of mismatched tarps, some duct-taped into place, some flapping lazily in the breeze like flags. A rusted weathervane spun uselessly, pointing in whatever direction it pleased.

Old crab pots and ragged fishing nets littered the front porch, along with a cracked cooler, a leaning stack of empty buckets, and a suspiciously broken recliner. A faded *No Trespassing* sign was nailed crookedly above the door, made less effective by the cheerful flip-flop doormat curling at the edges.

Maybe we shouldn't be going in there, it's technically breaking the law.

Even the windows looked tired—salt-smudged and

streaked. One was boarded over with a tabletop from a defunct local seafood restaurant. The faded logo of a smiling lobster was barely visible beneath peeling paint.

Cara swallowed hard. "Well, he always said he liked to live close to nature. I just didn't think it meant he was feral."

Marnie sniffed. "I've seen hoarder shows with more curb appeal."

They shared a glance, and the fleeting spark of humor did little to chase away Cara's dread. Darryl might've been a creep, but even his house seemed like it wanted no part in whatever mess he'd left behind. *It can't be worse, can it? He's already been killed.*

"Ready?" Marnie whispered, startling Cara from her thoughts.

Cara nodded, but her gaze lingered on the weather-beaten door. She wrapped her hand around the corroded knob, giving it a hesitant twist. To her surprise, it turned easily. "It's unlocked," she murmured.

"Maybe the police didn't bother to secure it? Seems unprofessional." Marnie said, though her tone carried little conviction.

Cara swallowed hard, a cold shiver crawling its way up her spine. She pushed the door open slowly, the hinges groaning in protest, and they stepped into the dim, stale-smelling shack.

The interior was dim and filled with neglect. The moment Cara crossed the threshold, the air thickened, heavy with the damp. Her eyes strained to adjust to the gloom; a shaft of dusty light slanted through the boarded window, catching the motes that drifted in slow, lazy spirals. She stepped forward cautiously, the warped floorboards groaning beneath her weight.

The place was a disorganized maze: an armchair with a burst seam spilling yellow stuffing, an old coffee table stained with drink rings, and piles of papers.

Marnie wasted no time, heading straight for a low cabinet near the back wall. She crouched, rifling through a box of tangled cords and yellowed receipts. "Check anywhere something could be hidden," she said without peering up. Her voice carried an urgency that felt *personal. What is* she *looking for?*

Cara's gaze swept over a half-collapsed bookshelf, where warped paperbacks leaned drunkenly against one another. She trailed her fingers along their ruined spines, then paused at a jar stuffed with loose change and rusted screws. Tugging her sleeve over her fingers, she curiously shifted it aside, revealing no obvious clues.

Moving along, her foot struck something under the couch with a hollow *thud*. She knelt, reached under the couch, and tugged a battered cigar box into the light. Inside, she found a few seashells, a folded map of the coastline with several locations circled in red ink, and a postcard depicting a cheerful lighthouse—its message side blank.

Marnie appeared at her shoulder, startling her. "Anything?"

Cara closed the lid and shook her head. "Not yet."

They had stepped into a time capsule. The remnants of Darryl's life were scattered about.

"Let's look for anything unusual," Cara suggested, her eyes scanning the room for clues.

As they rummaged through drawers and sifted through disheveled papers, Cara's thoughts buzzed with the events of the past few days. The quilters had started to unravel, and none more so than Marnie. Her defensive attitude, her quickness to shut down questions, and the way she had turned combative during the group argument, weighed heavily on Cara's mind. Marnie was hiding something, something that connected her to Darryl in ways none of the others suspected.

Cara moved a stack of papers aside and uncovered a pale conch shell behind them, its whorled surface dulled by a thin film of dust. The shell felt heavier than it should so she tilted it, listening for any noise inside. Her pulse kicked up, and a warning voice in her head whispered, *Don't do this. Not with her in the room.* But curiosity drowned out caution. She shook it again and it rattled faintly. Cara wedged her fingernails into the shell's spiral opening, and pulled a scrap of paper free. The paper was thin, almost translucent.

Unfolding it, she scanned the jagged handwriting:

Meet tonight. It's crucial. We can't let them find out.

Someone had met Darryl the night he died. And whoever 'they' were, the note's author feared them.

From across the room, Marnie's voice floated over. "Anything interesting over there?"

Cara flinched, nearly crumpling the paper in her fist. She glanced at Marnie, who was bent over a drawer, her back turned—but her shoulders were tense, angled like she might spin around at any second.

Refolding the note with deliberate care, Cara slid it into her pocket as though she were simply wiping her hands. "Just more junk," she lied.

The note was unsigned, but its meaning seemed obvious—someone had arranged to meet Darryl on the night he died. Cara's thoughts immediately flew to Marnie. The note seemed like the missing piece. *Who was meeting with Darryl. And why? I wonder if Marnie made up the dream just to have a reason to go to his house. Maybe even to destroy potential evidence. But why tell me? So I would be her alibi in case it went south and we got caught snooping? Or to perhaps point the finger at me later?*

"Let's get out of here," Cara said.

Marnie straightened from the drawer, dusting her hands on her jeans. "Fine. I've seen enough of this dump anyway." Her tone was brisk, but her gaze darted once toward Cara's pocket before sliding away again, quick as a pinprick.

Cara followed her toward the door.

Outside, gulls wheeled overhead.

"You know, Bean's always where she shouldn't be," Marnie said. "She just stumbles into things—maybe this time she stumbled into Darryl."

The sand shifted under Cara's shoes, each step sinking just enough to remind her how unsteady the ground between the retreat had become.

The rental's porch came into view, its weathered boards silvered by salt and spray. Cara trailed a hand along the railing as they climbed the steps. At this point, she couldn't say who she trusted anymore. Inside, the living room waited unchanged: quilts draped over chairs, the fabric stacked in piles, bags everywhere—the scene was exactly as they'd left it. And yet, the house no longer felt like a haven. Cara forced a yawn and rubbed at her eyes, a flimsy excuse to slip away. "I'm going to take a shower. I feel all sandy."

"All right, I'll make some more coffee," Marnie replied, her voice neutral. But to Cara, it sounded suspiciously detached.

Cara hurried to the bathroom, a nervous sweat becoming clammy on her skin. She closed the door, turned on the water, and pulled the note from her pocket. With shaking hands, she dialed Detective Thistlewitt's number.

"Detective Thistlewitt, it's Cara," she whispered when he picked up.

"Cara? What's going on?" His voice was sharp, instantly alert.

"I found something at Darryl's beach bungalow. A note. It was hidden in a conch shell. It says someone was supposed to meet him the night he died, but it's unsigned."

"You went back there?" Thistlewitt's tone sharpened. "Cara, that's still a crime scene."

"I know. But the place wasn't even locked, and I had to see for myself. You missed something—the note was hidden. If I hadn't gone, we wouldn't even know it existed."

A long silence stretched across the line before he replied. "You're lucky no one caught you there. I don't condone it, but I can't ignore the lead. Tell me exactly what it said."

"Unsigned," she repeated, her throat tight. "But someone must've met him that night."

"Do you have any idea who it could be?"

Cara hesitated.

She hadn't wanted to believe it, but Marnie's behavior had been too erratic, too defensive. The way she'd snapped at the others, the way she shut down any probing questions, and deflected blame on Bean—it all lined up.

She hesitated, not wanting to out her friend, but couldn't stop herself. "I think it was Marnie," Cara blurted. "She's been acting so strange lately. I don't want to believe it, and I have no proof, but something's not right."

"That's a serious accusation, Cara. Are you sure?"

"I'm not sure about anything anymore," Cara replied, a mixture of frustration and fear bubbling in her chest. "But I can't ignore how she's been acting. It's like she's hiding something. All the women are thinking it. And now, with this note . . ."

"Listen, Cara." Thistlewitt's voice took on a more urgent tone. "You need to be careful. If Marnie is involved—and I'm not saying she is, but if she is—things could get dangerous. Desperate people do desperate things. Keep your eyes open, and trust no one."

His words sent a shiver down Cara's spine. *She and I are sleeping under the same roof!*

With a huff, Cara turned off the water. The shower could wait. She needed a plan for Marnie without letting on that she had just called Detective Thistlewitt. Pulling herself together, she exited the bathroom, and crashed into Marnie, who was holding two oversized mugs of coffee.

"Whoa!" Marnie yelped as both mugs tipped over, splashing coffee down their shirts and onto the floor.

"Ugh, I'm so sorry!" Cara stammered, stepping back as the hot liquid soaked through her clothes.

Marnie glanced down at her now-coffee-stained sweater. "Well, that's just great," she grabbed a towel to mop up the mess. "You didn't even shower, Cara. What were you doing in there?"

Cara forced a shaky laugh, bending to help dab at the coffee pooling on the floor with another towel.

She had to think fast. "I—I was trying to decide if I had time to wash my hair," she lied. "Guess I took too long debating." She peered down at the mess of coffee. "Now I really do need a shower."

Marnie wrung out the towel over the sink and didn't seem convinced. She narrowed her eyes, her expression hardening further. "Is that so?" she mumbled under her breath but loud enough for Cara to hear. "You know, I've been wondering if *you* had something to do with Darryl's death."

Cara's stomach dropped. "Excuse me?"

"*I said*, I've been wondering," Marnie repeated, her voice louder, more accusatory. "You've been acting weird since this all started. And now you're coming out of the bathroom with no shower and a bunch of lame excuses? It's all a bit suspicious, don't you think?"

"Marnie, what the heck are you talking about? I've been trying to figure out *who* killed Darryl—just like everyone else! You're the one who's been acting defensive and weird. You're hiding something, and it's making *me* wonder if there's more to *your* story."

The argument had grown louder. Haze and Bean stumbled out of their rooms, blinking groggily.

"What's going on?" Bean asked, rubbing her eyes.

Cara's frustration boiled over. She pulled the crumpled note from her pocket and held it up for everyone to see. "This! This is what's going on!" she shouted. "I found this at Darryl's beach shack. It was hidden inside a conch shell. It says someone was supposed to meet him the night he died, but it's unsigned. And I'm starting to think Marnie knows more about it than she's letting on!"

Marnie's eyes widened in shock. "What? Cara, are you serious?"

"Yes, I am!" Cara snapped. "You're so quick to shut down any questions about Darryl. Why? What aren't you telling us?"

Bean and Haze exchanged wary glances.

Marnie's face flushed with anger. "I'm not hiding anything. I had nothing to do with his death and I didn't meet him that night!"

"Then why all the secrets? Why the attitude? Why can't you just be honest with us?" Cara pressed, trembling with frustration and suspicion.

The conversation collapsed into a brittle reticence, the women watching her carefully. Cara held the note in her hand.

Before Marnie could respond, a sudden knock at the door rattled the air between them.

Everyone froze and a knock came again.

Cara's gaze darted toward the kitchen windows. All she saw were shifting shadows, distorted by the morning light. "Who's that?" she asked but no one answered.

A third knock followed—this one so forceful it rattled the thin doorframe.

"It's too early for the police to just show up," Bean said as she edged toward the hallway, as if distance could shield her. "What if it's not the police?"

Then—three slow, deliberate taps. Almost polite.

A pressure tightened in her ribs, making it hard to breathe. *Whoever it is knows we are inside.*

"Who's there?" Marnie called out, shakily.

There was no answer. Just more knocking.

They weren't expecting anyone as far as she knew— especially not at this early hour. Cara's thoughts spiraled, imagining the worst. *Could it be someone trying to shut us up for getting too close to the truth? Is this connected to the note?*

After a long, tense pause, a voice came through the door—gruff but familiar.

"It's Detective Thistlewitt."

Cara exhaled, but the relief was short-lived. *Is he here to arrest Marnie? On my hunch?*

CHAPTER 9

knots in the storyline

Detective Thistlewitt stood in the doorway, his figure imposing in the early morning light. *Did my phone call seal my friend's fate?*

Marnie, Bean, Haze, and Trudy all stared at the detective with varying degrees of surprise and apprehension. The note was still clutched in Cara's hand, and she quickly tucked it into her pocket, suddenly unsure if she wanted to give it to him just yet.

"What brings you here so early, Detective?" Marnie's tone was guarded, her eyes darting to Cara for a split second before she turned back to him.

"I thought I'd stop by," Thistlewitt said, stepping over the threshold without waiting for an invitation. "I've got a few more questions for everyone. And it seems like now might be a good time to address a few inconsistencies."

The detective's gaze swept over the group, lingering on

Cara as if he was acknowledging her for being the one to reach out to him. He nodded. "Shall we sit?"

They moved like chess pieces. Marnie claimed the corner of the overstuffed corduroy couch, her body angled toward the door. Bean sank into the far end of the same couch, tucking her legs under her and folding her arms tight across her chest. Haze chose the chair nearest the hallway—a subtle barricade—her gaze fixed on some invisible spot in the carpet. Trudy perched on the ottoman, knees together, hands clasped, eyes darting between the detective and the rest of the group.

Cara stayed standing for a moment longer, scanning the space as if it might tell her where to sit. The faint, stale aroma of the early morning's coffee still clung to the air, mingling with the sharper scent of fabric sizing. Quilt scraps were scattered across the coffee table like misplaced evidence, a pincushion sat in the middle like a paperweight. The steady tick of the wall clock filled the silence, every second feeling louder than the last until she finally sank into the cushion beside Bean, acutely aware of how far she was from the door.

Her stomach churned. *I started all of this.* Her call to Thistlewitt had obviously stirred things up. *It's too late to turn back now.* The others watched her, suspicion darkening their eyes.

Thistlewitt remained standing and took in the arrangement without comment at first, but his gaze flicked from one woman to the next in quick, precise movements. He paused and locked eyes with Marnie, and glanced down the narrow hall at Haze's back. "Let's get right to it. Cara, I understand you've been doing a little investigating on your own. Why don't you share with the group what you've found?"

Cara's fingers twitched toward her pocket, where the crumpled note sat like a hot coal. *I can't believe he outed me!*

She scowled as she slowly withdrew it, then handed it to the detective, her throat dry. "I found this at Darryl's beach shack. It was hidden in a conch shell. It suggests someone was supposed to meet him the night he died."

The room erupted into murmurs of denial, each quilter protesting, but Thistlewitt stilled them with a wave of his hand.

"That's not all," Cara added, her voice shaky but determined. She stared directly at Marnie. "Every time I ask about Darryl, you shut down or change the subject. It feels like you're hiding something."

Marnie stood, her body trembling with rage. "*Hiding something*? Are you serious? If anyone here has been acting suspicious, it's you, Cara! You're the one who's been sneaking around and making secret phone calls to the detective!"

"That's enough," Thistlewitt interrupted, calmly but with an authoritative edge. "I'm here to uncover the truth, and we're going to do this systematically." He turned to Marnie, pointing at her. "You first."

Marnie leaned back into the couch, arms folded, chin

tilted defiantly. "Fine. Ask your questions. I've nothing to hide."

The detective stepped forward, his pen poised over his notebook. "What was your relationship with Darryl? And don't just give me the surface details—what's the real story?"

Marnie waved the questions away with her hand. "Darryl and I were . . . complicated. We had some history. He borrowed money from me a few years ago and never paid it back. It wasn't a huge sum, but enough to cause some friction between us. But that's all it was—friction. I didn't kill him over a few hundred dollars."

Thistlewitt said, "You realize, Mrs. Kessler, that half of communication is body language. And yours is screaming *I'd rather be anywhere else.*"

Marnie gave a humorless laugh. "Maybe because I don't like being accused of murder during my vacation and before I've even had my second cup of coffee."

He continued, "Or maybe because you're holding back. When was the last time you spoke to Darryl alone?"

"A week ago. Before the retreat started."

"Interesting. I've been told you two argued at the dock a few weeks ago."

Marnie's lips thinned. "It wasn't an argument. He owed me money and I reminded him. That had nothing to do with this." She shifted in her seat, uncrossing and recrossing her legs, and shrugged. "That's it."

He turned to Bean. "Your turn."

Bean sat up straighter, then immediately slouched,

twisting her sleep shirt in her lap. "Look, I didn't like Darryl, but *I* didn't kill him."

"Where were you after the bonfire?" Thistlewitt said casually.

"It was just for a minute. And I didn't go far—not even to the dunes. Just to get some air."

"Alone?"

Bean hesitated. "Yes. No. I—" She forced a laugh. "This is ridiculous. It wasn't me."

Haze leaned forward from her armchair, voice cool. "You're making too much of it, Detective. Bean was here all night. We would have noticed if she went *wandering* long enough to kill someone."

"Would you?" Thistlewitt asked without looking at her. "Wouldn't you just cover for her?"

Was Haze protecting Bean...or herself? A leaden weight settled in her chest as she glanced around at each of them. "Can't you all see? We're tearing each other apart. And for what? We're all suspects now. No one's above suspicion."

The detective's gaze lingered on the bookshelf in the corner, the clock, then the pile of fabric swatches on the table. "Security cameras will confirm it."

The conversation died on the spot. Cara blinked. "Wait . . . there's security cameras along the beach?"

He offered a faint smile and tipped his head in agreement. For the first time, Cara felt the gears shift. She may have underestimated him. He wasn't just there to smile and ask questions and bust their chops. He was watching and stitching it all together.

CHAPTER 10

thistlewitt's theory

The sun beamed through the windows and across the enormous braided rug in the open-concept living room where the quilters were gathered. The noose of suspicion had tightened around them.

Detective Thistlewitt leaned against the back of the kitchen island facing the living room area again, arms crossed, his expression unreadable. He had listened intently as the women argued, each of them slinging accusations. Now, the quilters were scattered. Trudy quietly fumed at the back door of the kitchen. Cara's shoulders ached from the tension winding tighter with every second. No one met her eyes, and Marnie's cleared name hadn't made them safer—it had simply made someone else guiltier.

"I think we're dealing with something bigger here," Thistlewitt said.

Cara blinked at him, confused. *Is he accusing all of us?*

Or is this some calculated bluff meant to see who cracks first? "What do you mean?" she asked.

Giving her a long look before pushing off the counter, he walked to the middle of the room, commanding everyone's attention. "I don't believe any of you are acting alone. From the beginning, this case had too many loose ends—alibis that almost, but didn't quite, fit."

Haze's lips pressed into a thin line. Marnie shifted in her seat. The air carried a hint of Thistlewitt's aftershave.

"What if you're all protecting someone? Or maybe, each other?"

The hairs on the back of Cara's neck pricked as his gaze landed squarely on her. *Does he suspect me?*

His words were thick with implication. The quilters exchanged glances, surprise and indignation crossing their faces.

Marnie was the first to speak. "We've barely been able to stand each other since Darryl died. You think we're all in this together?"

The detective's jaw tightened. "I've seen this before. A group dynamic where each person thinks they're covering up for a friend, not knowing that they're part of something much darker."

Cara's stomach twisted. "These are my friends. You can't really think we're all involved in something sinister?"

The detective's gaze softened slightly, but he didn't waver. "Cara, I know it's hard to accept. But the evidence is pointing in a direction you might not like."

She shook her head. "We may have our differences, but

there's no way any of them—any of us—would kill someone." she said with a conviction that she herself didn't truly believe.

He raised an eyebrow. "What about the note you found? Or the secrets you've all been keeping about Darryl?"

Cara bristled. "Those secrets are personal, not criminal."

"Personal can turn criminal real fast," he replied, his tone measured but firm.

Cara flinched at the intensity of Marnie's declaration. She wanted to believe her friend. She wanted to believe *all of them*. But the detective's calm, logical approach was forcing her to see things she hadn't noticed before.

Marnie zeroed in on Bean. "Oh, please. If anyone, it was you, Bean. Always lingering near his table at the guild, laughing at every dumb joke like it was the first time you'd heard it."

Bean's mouth dropped open. "That's not fair! I laugh at *everyone's* dumb jokes. It's called being polite." Her cheeks flushed a blotchy pink, and her hands knotted together. "I was just trying to be kind and friendly."

"Friendly?" Marnie laughed, short and sharp. "He wasn't exactly the type who deserved your sweetness."

Across the room, Trudy scoffed under her breath. Haze's head snapped in her direction. "Don't start, Trudy."

Trudy lifted her chin, eyes narrowing. "I just think

some people like having an audience. Makes them feel important."

"Better than disappearing every time things get tense," Haze shot back.

Cara held up a hand, breaking the volley. "What pattern?" she asked Thistlewitt.

"Every one of you had something to lose if Darryl started talking. Marnie with the money issue. Bean with her *kindness that looked a little too much like sympathy in the wrong company.* Trudy with her past."

Hesitating for a moment, he sighed then continued, "I did some digging. Darryl wasn't just some harmless dude, or a quilter for that matter. He may have had some shady business connections. And Trudy, here, wasn't always the sweet, unassuming quilter she seems to be."

Cara's mind stumbled, trying to reconcile the Trudy she knew—pastel sweaters, cheerful giggle, cupcakes balanced on floral plates—with the version Thistlewitt hinted at.

Trudy shifted. "I—" she began, her voice trembling just enough for Cara to hear it.

Even Marnie, usually quick to scoff, leaned forward slightly, as if she didn't want to miss a word.

A spark of satisfaction flickered across Thistlewitt's face—brief, but unmistakable. It seemed like he'd wanted this ripple of doubt and he had achieved it.

Trudy's face drained of color and she didn't protest. Her lips parted, then pressed shut again as if she were choosing her words from a minefield. "That was years ago," she said, her tone fragile around the edges. "A mistake I already paid for."

"Let's not pretend, Trudy," he said quietly.

Marnie stiffened, shoulders drawn back. Bean leaned forward.

"I know about the small claims suit involving that business deal with Darryl. You thought it was buried, but Darryl knew more than he let on, didn't he? That's why you've been so tense."

The room fell into another shocked silence, and Cara's stomach dropped. *Trudy never mentioned any of this.* Her sweet, soft-spoken friend, involved in a business deal with Darryl? *It doesn't make sense, and yet . . . it fits with the detective's theory.*

Trudy shook her head, then, her voice trembling, she spoke. "It—it wasn't like that. Yes, we had a disagreement about a business venture years ago, but that was over. We hadn't spoken about it in ages."

Thistlewitt gave her a long look. "Maybe not. But Darryl had a way of keeping tabs on people, didn't he? And now he's dead. Coincidence?"

Cara's head swam. The more he spoke, the more her carefully constructed view of her friends began to crumble.

"I can't believe this," Cara murmured, pacing the room. "There's no way all of this is connected. There's no way *they*"—she gestured to her friends—"could be involved in something like this."

The detective continued, "Sometimes, it's the people closest to us we know the least about. You don't want to believe it, but the evidence doesn't lie. We're missing one final piece of the puzzle, and I think it has to do with Darryl's finances."

"What about them?" Cara asked.

He reached into his coat and pulled out a slim folder. "I got hold of Darryl's financial records. He had some . . . unexpected expenses. Large sums of money going out. And I think one of your friends had something to do with it."

Cara, weak in the knees, asked, "Who?"

He opened the folder, flipping through the pages until he landed on a document. His finger traced the numbers, and his brow furrowed. "There's another pattern here," he said, glancing up at Cara and the rest of the quilters. "Someone was paying Darryl a significant amount of money on a regular basis. And it started around the same time that he began working more closely with your quilting group."

Bean finally spoke up from her seat by the window, her voice strained. "What are you saying? Are you implying one of us was blackmailing Darryl?"

"Not blackmail, necessarily." He shook his head. "But it looks like Darryl had leverage over someone. He was receiving large sums of money, but he wasn't reporting it. Whoever was paying him wasn't doing it legally."

Cara's pulse thundered in her ears. *One of my friends, paying Darryl off.* She tried to wrap her head around the idea but kept coming up short, but there was Trudy's receipt.

As if sensing Cara's thoughts, Trudy shifted uncomfortably, her earlier defiance beginning to falter. "Darryl knew things. About people's pasts. He wasn't an honest man. He's always been involved in some pretty shady stuff, as far as I know. So, if someone thought he might talk?"

"Exactly. And it wasn't just about quilting or a minor dispute. I suspect Darryl was involved in something much bigger. And *whoever* paid him was either trying to keep him quiet or keep their own secrets buried," Marnie offered.

The thought of Darryl holding something over her friends, using it to manipulate them, was awful. "But . . . Why would they go as far as to kill him? And why now?"

Thistlewitt's eyes softened as he glared at Cara. "Sometimes, people do desperate things when they feel cornered. You know that as well as anyone."

A lump rose in her throat. It wasn't just the shock of Darryl's death or the revelation about her friends. This went deeper than she could have ever imagined.

"But we still don't know who," Cara whispered, her voice shaky.

Thistlewitt glanced down at the folder once more and pulled out a final sheet of paper, handing it to her. "I have a strong suspicion. One last piece of the puzzle. The person who had the most to lose, and the one Darryl was squeezing the hardest. This document shows a business transaction—a large sum paid to Darryl right before his death. It's tied to a company that has connections to someone here."

Cara's hand trembled as she took the paper and scanned the text. She didn't want to believe it, but the evidence was clear. She recognized the name listed on the financial records.

"Bean?" She gasped, peering up at her friend sitting by the window. "This can't be right." Cara searched for the warm, easy smile that always made the group feel lighter—but it wasn't there. Bean's skin had gone the color of bleached muslin. *Both Bean and Trudy were paying him.*

The sea wind rattled the window behind Bean, a hollow, restless sound. Across the room, Marnie chortled and relief flickered across her face.

"No." Haze said flatly, but she didn't elaborate. She didn't even look at Bean.

If Trudy or Bean are guilty . . . will I have the courage to help Thistlewitt prove it?

"I didn't mean for it to go this far," Bean said.

CHAPTER 11

a thread of guilt

The room grew colder. Bean, once so strong and confident, now appeared small and fragile, her hands clasped tightly in her lap, as if she were trying to hold herself together. Cara ached as her friend unraveled before her eyes.

No one spoke. Even the gentle rush of waves beyond the glass seemed sharper than before.

Detective Thistlewitt stood quietly by the door, his face a mask of professionalism. It seemed he had been closing in on Bean all along, and now, with the evidence in hand, there was nothing left but to make the arrest.

His voice was calm but firm as he stepped forward. "Bean, it's time we had a conversation down at the station. I'm going to have to take you in."

Bean's eyes darted around the room, as if searching for an escape, for someone to defend her. "This isn't happening. I didn't kill Darryl," she stammered, her voice cracking with panic. "I didn't! I just wanted him to stop. I was scared—scared of what he would do if people found out."

A jittery rush swept through her. She wanted to leap to her friend's defense, to tell Thistlewitt he had it wrong. But the folder, the numbers, the way Bean's gaze kept skittering away—it all weighed heavy on Cara. She searched Bean's face for the small signs she'd come to recognize over years of friendship: the tiny crease between her brows, the quick press of lips, the way her shoulders curled inward when she was hiding something. They were all there.

Across the room, Trudy's frown deepened.

Cara swallowed hard. *Am I fighting for her because she's innocent? Or because I can't face what it means if she's not?* If Bean was guilty, the number of people Cara could trust had just shrunk to none. "Bean, what did he have on you? Why didn't you tell us?"

Bean's eyes met Cara's, and for a moment, her defenses crumbled. Tears welled up, and she shook her head slowly. "I didn't think you'd understand. Darryl . . . he found out about some bad decisions I made years ago. Business deals that went south."

Her voice faltered, but she pushed on. "At first, it wasn't blackmail. He made it sound harmless—said he needed a loan, just until his next big deal. I thought I was helping him. Then the requests started coming more often. Higher amounts. He didn't ask anymore—he told me. Said he'd make sure certain mistakes came to light if I didn't pay up."

Cara's mind flashed to Bean's quilt shop—walls lined

with neatly stacked bolts of fabric, the hum of the sewing machines in the back, customers chatting at the counter. The thought of losing it would gut Bean.

Bean's voice broke. "I told myself it would be the last payment every single time. But it never was. He had this way of looking at me like he already owned the truth, and that sooner or later, he'd make sure everyone else did too."

Bean had been having distracted moments as well. All the little things Cara had brushed off now slid into place, forming a picture she didn't want to see.

"Why didn't you trust me? Trust us? We would've helped," said Cara.

"I didn't want to drag anyone else into this mess," Bean choked out, tears spilling down her face. "I thought I could handle it. I thought if I just paid him off, he'd let it go. But he kept asking for more. I was desperate."

Thistlewitt gave her a long, measured look. "That doesn't explain why Darryl ended up dead, Bean. We know about the payments, but was there more? Did things get out of control?"

Bean's lip trembled, and she buried her face in her hands. "I didn't kill him. I swear I didn't! I went to confront him the night he died, but by the time I got there... he was already dead and I panicked. I thought no one would believe me. I thought they'd think I did it because of the money, because of everything. So I... I ran back here and went to bed."

Doubt gnawed within Cara. *Can Bean really be innocent? Or just another attempt to cover tracks?*

The detective's handcuffs gleamed. "Bean, you're under arrest for suspicion of murder and obstruction of justice."

Bean's head snapped up, her eyes wide with terror. "No, please, you can't—"

Cara stepped back, her stomach twisting in knots as the detective gently but firmly cuffed Bean's tiny wrists. The reality of the situation hit Cara like a tidal wave. *Bean, my friend, is going to jail.*

"I didn't do it," Bean repeated, her voice breaking as Thistlewitt guided her toward the door. "Please, Cara, you have to believe me. I didn't kill him!"

Cara wanted to respond, but she had no words. The room spun around her as Bean's tear-streaked face, a portrait of anguish, disappeared through the doorway. Thistlewitt's steady grip guided her out and the latch clicked behind them.

Marnie laughed. Short and bitter, it sounded more like a cough. "Guess we know who not to save a seat for at the next retreat," she barked, but the sharpness in her voice faded almost instantly. Her lips pressed together, like she wanted to snatch the words back.

Trudy paced a slow loop from the window to the couch and back again, arms wrapped tightly around herself. She dropped into one of the seats with a *thud*.

Cara peered at the empty spot where Bean had been sitting. The indentation in the cushion was still there.

No one looked at each other. Cara's world had irrevocably changed. Bean was gone.

Relief, sorrow, and guilt swirled inside her, leaving her raw and uncertain. *Did I do the right thing by pushing for the truth? Or did I just destroy the one friendship I believed in the most?*

Marnie stared at the floor, her face pale, while Trudy's usual cheer had curdled like she might explode from the tension.

"I never thought it would be her," Trudy whispered, breaking the silence. "I thought . . . I don't know what I thought. But not Bean."

Marnie sighed, her voice hollow. "None of us did. We trusted her."

The words cut deep, and Cara's throat tightened. She trusted Bean too. And now, she didn't know what to believe anymore.

Thistlewitt's words replayed in her mind: "It's the people closest to us we know the least about."

Maybe he's right, but how can that possibly be? But if Bean didn't do it, then the killer is still out there—or in here?

CHAPTER 12

twist in the stitch

The retreat ended in quiet stillness, and the following days blurred together in a haze of uncertainty. The small coastal town buzzed with news of Bean's arrest, whispers following Cara wherever she went. At the quilt shop, the camaraderie seemed shattered.

Cara replayed Bean's words—how her friend had insisted she was innocent, how she had sworn she wasn't involved in Darryl's death. And though all the evidence pointed to her, something didn't sit right with Cara. *What if Bean was telling the truth?*

What if there was more to the story, a final piece of the puzzle that had yet to reveal itself. The tide was lower than the last time she'd been there with Marnie. Cara stepped over a scatter of driftwood and moved toward the shack, the salt air heavy.

They'd already searched Darryl's shack but something didn't sit right.

Cara wasn't sure if it was intuition, guilt, or just plain stubbornness—but she'd barely slept. And the way Darryl's name kept circling in her thoughts like a gull waiting for scraps made her wonder if they'd missed something.

The wind rattled the warped siding as she pried open the door again. It stuck, then gave way with a reluctant groan.

The same rank smell of mildew and salt and rot hung in the air like a stain that couldn't be scrubbed out. Cara's boots crunched across the warped floorboards as she moved, aimless at first, then circling.

She tried to picture him here—Darryl. Greasy hair, yellow teeth, that smug laugh. The way he talked down to everyone. The way he preyed on kindness, twisted it into leverage. Her jaw clenched.

Bean didn't deserve this.

None of them did.

Cara stared down at the rusted file cabinet in the corner. She'd seen the file cabinet before—rusted open and dented. Nothing inside but a broken radio.

"Where would a coward stash his secrets?"

Anger flared again, and she kicked the bottom of the cabinet, hard. Metal clanged against metal. Then there was a *pop*. Cara dropped to her knees. A small panel at the base jostled loose. The cabinet had a false bottom. Her fingers found the seam and tugged, lifting it free.

She found a manilla envelope, folded once and stuffed deep. Tugging out, she unfolded it carefully. A few crumpled payment slips fell into her lap, along with torn receipts and a single folded scrap of paper. One line, scrawled in jagged ink, stopped her cold:

FINAL PAYMENT FROM M—THAT'S *what she thinks.*

The ocean crashed in the distance. A jolt ran through her, tightening her chest. The "M" had to be Marnie. Her friend hadn't told the full truth. But Darryl likely would not have stopped.

Her grip shook on the keys as she stumbled into the driver's seat and pulled the door shut hard behind her. Cara drove toward the one place she had avoided since the arrest—Marnie's house. Streetlights cast pale pools of light over the quiet neighborhood, each one flickering past like a metronome for her racing thoughts.

It wasn't Bean.

She gripped the steering wheel tighter.

One of her friends had indeed been pulling the strings all along. *Using Bean as a distraction, as a scapegoat.*

Cara's mind replayed every conversation, every tense glance and half-truth, the puzzle pieces rearranging themselves into a picture she didn't want to see.

The roads blurred together in the short, tense drive. Familiar houses passed in a haze, their windows glowing warmly, a stark contrast to the storm of suspicion brewing inside her. She slowed as Marnie's house came into view, the quiet suburban street eerily still. When she pulled into the driveway, the house was mostly dark, its shadowed windows giving nothing away—except for a dim light glowing faintly in the living room. Cara climbed the steps and knocked on the door, her knuckles rapping anxiously against the wood.

Footsteps shuffled on the other side and then Marnie opened the door. "Cara? What are you doing here?"

"I know the truth, Marnie," Cara said, her voice steady, despite the storm of emotions inside her. "It wasn't Bean who killed Darryl. It was you." Cara pointed a finger of accusation at her supposed friend who had just stood by and let Bean take the fall for her actions.

Marnie's face went slack. "That's absurd."

Cara locked eyes with Marnie's. "You were the one paying Darryl. You were the one who needed him gone. The money Bean owed wasn't the only thing he had on someone."

Marnie's face paled, but she didn't move. "You have no proof."

"I found a note. I know you were the one he was squeezing."

"That doesn't prove anything." Marnie turned away quickly. "Lots of people were paying Darryl money. Bean. Trudy. Maybe even you."

"No. Not me. Don't deflect. I know you're the one. The note said: *M* and that's all the proof *I* need." Cara stepped into the house. "He never planned to stop, did he?"

"You're making assumptions." But her voice wavered.

"Marnie," Cara said quietly.

With her hands curled into fists at her side, Marnie opened her mouth, shut it, then said, "Because I'm tired." The words exhaled like air leaking from a balloon. "Tired of pretending I've had everything under control, of jumping every time someone mentions his name."

She sank into an armchair. "I didn't mean to kill him. I just wanted him to stop. He kept asking for more and more money. And threatening to tell the guild, the press, anyone and everyone he thought would listen. I thought if I scared him, if I could show him I wasn't bluffing . . . but then he lunged at me, and I—" She buried her face in her hands. "It got out of control. And when I saw Bean had gone to meet him, too, I panicked. What if she knew? I thought it would all unravel. Yes, I let it happen, let the police think it was her."

Grief and disbelief pressed against Cara's chest. *This isn't the Marnie I know.*

Or maybe it was—and she'd just never looked closely enough. Her oldest friend, the woman she had trusted, had been hiding a deadly secret all along. "Why didn't you come forward?"

Marnie glanced up, her eyes filled with tears. "I couldn't. I was in too deep. I knew they'd arrest me. I would have lost everything. My whole life . . . It would've all been over. Until I saw a way out by letting her take the blame. I knew she was innocent and they would discover that." She twisted her hands in her lap "I'm so sorry, Cara. I didn't want it to come to this."

Cara had wanted answers, but this betrayal was too much to bear, and the emotion gutted her. "You let Bean go to jail for something you did," Cara said, her voice shaking with fury and shock.

"I panicked!" Marnie cried, standing up suddenly. "I didn't know what else to do. I thought if she was arrested, it would all be over. But it's not, is it? *You* had to keep digging."

"I'm calling the detective."

Marnie's face crumpled, the last shred of her defenses falling away. "Please, Cara, don't. I'll confess. I'll tell him everything. Just . . . don't make it worse than it already is."

Cara's hand shook as she pulled out her phone and dialed Detective Thistlewitt's number. Marnie sank to her knees, sobbing. Her friend had committed a crime, and had betrayed their trust. And now, nothing would ever be the same.

By the time Thistlewitt arrived, the house was quiet, save for the soft sound of her broken friend's continued weeping. Cara stood in the corner, numb and exhausted. The detective took Marnie into custody, reading her her rights as she was led out the door.

epilogue: together again

Weeks had passed since Marnie's arrest, but for Cara, it might as well have been a lifetime. The group had settled into a strange pattern of avoidance. Quilting, once a joyful escape, had become something else—an emblem of all that had unraveled. She hadn't touched a needle or thread since the day the detective took Marnie away.

It was a cloudy, drab morning when Cara returned at last to the quilt shop. The familiar feel of fabric was soft and comforting as she glided her hand over the new arrivals. A few guild members sat at their usual spots, but the laughter and chatter that had once filled the room was noticeably absent.

Haze sat at the end of the cutting table, rotary blade in hand, and a distant stare. The usual precision in her work had been replaced with a cautious slowness, like she was thinking too hard about each cut.

Bean hovered by a circular rack of fabric bolts,

clutching a bundle of batik fat quarters to her chest. She appeared zombie-like.

"Hey," Haze said gently, not peering up from her fabric.

Bean's voice faltered. "Hi, I . . . wasn't sure if I should come."

Haze paused mid-cut and looked up this time, frowning. She finished the cut, then set the rotary cutter down with a soft click, closed the blade, and finally met Bean's eyes.

"You belong here," she said simply.

Bean swallowed. "I don't feel like I do."

Haze stood and crossed over to her, folding her arms. "Look, I'm not going to pretend I wasn't angry. Or scared. Or confused. But I know what Darryl was capable of. He used guilt like some people use scissors. I know he was capable of cutting someone to ribbons until they barely recognized themself."

Cara went to Bean, as well. Bean's eyes welled, and she blinked fast. "I should've trusted you all. I should've come clean earlier. But I thought . . . I thought if I handled it alone, I'd protect you."

"We don't need protection from each other," Haze said, looking to Cara for confirmation. She nodded. "We need honesty. Even if it's messy."

"Well, lucky for you, I'm really good at messy." Bean laughed. "Do you think the others in the guild will forgive me?"

"They're quilters, Bean. We're built to mend. Just give

them time." She shrugged. "And maybe don't bring shrimp salad to the next retreat."

Bean chuckled, a really sweet laugh this time. "Deal."

Cara reached out a hand to Bean's arm and was met with Bean's thin fingers, still clutching the fat quarter bundle like a talisman.

They stood there a moment longer, surrounded by bolts of fabric and pattern displays.

Then Haze plucked one bolt from the display, and raised an eyebrow. "Tie-dye dolphins?"

"Sounds like a challenge," Bean replied, grinning. "We can call them our *Funkadelic* quilts."

Haze smiled. "Welcome back, Bean."

Bean had been released after Marnie's confession, but the scars of the accusation still lingered between Bean and the other quilters. Cara hadn't even spoken to Bean since, and now, Cara and Bean took seats at a work table, and for a long moment, neither of them spoke.

"I didn't think I'd ever come back." Bean's was quiet, almost tentative.

"I wasn't sure I would either." Cara took a deep breath, searching for the right words. "I'm sorry, Bean. For everything, for doubting you and not seeing what was really happening. I should've trusted you."

Bean peered up at her with kind, tired eyes. "You didn't know. None of us did. Marnie was your oldest friend—she fooled all of us."

Nodding through the guilt while setting up her sewing machine, Cara replied, "I keep thinking . . . if I'd just paid closer attention. Or asked the right questions sooner, maybe this could've ended differently."

"Maybe. But the truth is, Darryl would've kept pushing, stirring things up until someone broke. It was only a matter of time." From a brightly colored bag, Bean unearthed a sewing machine sculpted into the shape of skeletal arm bones and plonked it onto the table. The foot pedal was a miniature tombstone, and the spool pin was a bony finger.

Cara blinked. "Bean. What in the Day-of-the-Dead disco nightmare is that?"

Bean grinned proudly. "My limited edition *Stitcher of the Damned*. It glows in the dark too!" she squealed.

"I'm terrified and impressed."

"And it growls like a tiny banshee when you jam the bobbin."

Cara laughed in spite of herself. "You brought *that* to your comeback sew-in?"

"Figured if I was going to rise from the ashes, I might as well bring a phoenix with LED lights and skeletal charm."

Cara smiled, the tightness in her chest loosening a little. "You really are excellent."

"Even when people forget it," Bean said with a soft smile.

"Marnie made the wrong choice," Cara said softly. "But she's still our friend too. Or . . . she was. I don't know what to call her now."

Bean sighed. "Maybe just someone we loved who lost

her way. That doesn't mean we stop loving her. Forgiveness doesn't mean forgetting—it just means we stop letting the hurt decide what comes next."

"I guess we start over now," Cara replied, glancing around the quilt shop. "Pick up the pieces and stitch a new story."

Bean smiled gently, her eyes crinkling. "Isn't that what quilters do best?"

Did you know? Reader reviews are very important to an indie author's success? They validate our work and help others find our stories. If you enjoyed Beach Brawl, please leave a happy review filled with stars.

http://Amazon.com/review/create-review?&asin=B0DGYN5C3J

As an added thank you, here's a free gift! Click here to tell me where to send it.
https://BookHip.com/PDJMNBR

meet the characters - cara

Cara Abbott
The mediator and reluctant sleuth.

- Observant, level-headed, and emotionally intelligent.
- Tends to avoid conflict but can't help stepping in when things feel off.
- Holds onto guilt and worries about group harmony.
- Deeply loyal—even when she's unsure who to trust.

Late 50s, short, with a practical, slightly tousled silver bob that never quite behaves near the sea.

Wears slacks, sensible sandals, and always has mismatched socks and earrings (a nervous habit when fiddled with).

meet the characters - bean

Bean (Short for Benjamin, a boys name which she hates)
The optimist.

- Cheerful, dreamy, and forever distracted by her next quirky quilt idea.
- Oblivious to tension—until it hits her like a flying pincushion.
- Talks too much when she's nervous.
- Loves fun over function and has *big ideas*, not always follow-through.
- Believes everything is better with sparkle, snacks, or stitching.

Early 60s, tall and lanky with wild, frizzy red curls always escaping her sun hat.

Dresses in bright colors and novelty quilting T-shirts with sayings like "Quilt Happens."

Generally stained somewhere (coffee, salsa, mystery food). She doesn't care what or where.

meet the characters - haze

Haze (Short for Hazel)
   The realist.

- Practical, organized, and always three steps ahead.
- Uses dry humor to defuse drama.
- Unshakable in a crisis—but has zero tolerance for nonsense.
- Finishes everything she starts, and resents those who don't.

Late 50s, petite with sharp features and short black hair cut in a sleek stacked bob.

Dresses in classic neutrals and perfectly pressed linen—makes even a smock look fashionable.

Wears a digital quilting ruler watch and is never without a notebook of fabric swatches.

meet the characters - marnie

Marnie
The skeptic and sassmaster.

- Sharp-tongued, fiercely independent, and a little insecure under all that attitude.
- Quick to criticize, but it's often a defense mechanism.
- Secretly worries what people think of her.
- Deep down, values the group more than she admits.
- Never admits she's wrong . . . at least, not out loud.

Around 60, fuller figure with big expressive eyes and a dramatic streak she tries to pass off as "practical flair."

Has thick, espresso-brown hair pulled into a no-nonsense twist that somehow still looks expensive—possibly because it is. Her brown eyes are match her hair.

Her lipstick game? Bold. Her eyebrow arch? Sharper than her tongue.

Smells faintly of lavender and frustration.

meet the characters - trudy

Trudy
The sunshine spinner.

- Perpetually cheerful, even when everything's falling apart.
- Avoids uncomfortable truths by fibbing, redirecting, or offering baked goods.
- Plays peacemaker but also plays dumb when she's hiding something.
- Often underestimated—sometimes by design.

Mid-60s, round-faced with a perpetual smile and soft, puffed-up strawberry blonde curls (set weekly). And bright blue eyes.

Wears pastel capris, embroidered cardigans.

Her quilt bag is monogrammed and her water bottle sparkles.

She giggles often—but not always for the reasons you'd think.

additional books

Award-winning author of the best-selling quilting cozy mystery series:

Sewing Suspicion - 2021 Indie Cozy Mystery Book of The Year Quilting Calamity - 2022 Indie Cozy Mystery Book of The Year

Inspired by the laugh-out-loud and fanciful aspects of cozies, Kathryn writes lighthearted, humorous mysteries that play on her passion for the craft of quilting.

She's a creative force in the quilting world. A talented pattern designer and storyteller, she blends her passion for textiles with her love of mystery and heartwarming tales. Through both her sewing patterns and fiction novels, Kathryn inspires quilters and readers alike to embrace creativity, community, and connection.

www.authorkathrynmykel.com

ADDITIONAL BOOKS

Quilting Cozy Mystery Series:

Sewing Suspicion (Book 1)
Quilting Calamity (Book 2)
Pressing Matters (Book 3)
Mutterly Mistaken
(Holiday Pet Sleuths Series) (Book 3.5)
Threading Trouble (Book 4)
Paw-in-Law
(Holiday Pet Sleuths Series) (Book 4.5)
Stitching Concerns (Book 5)
Purrfect Perpetrator
(Holiday Pet Sleuths Series) (Book 5.5)

ADDITIONAL BOOKS

Mending Mischief (Book 6)
Doggone Disaster
(Holiday Pet Sleuths Series) (Book 6.5)
Patchwork Perils (Book 7)
Seaming Uncertainty (Book 8)
~ Coming Soon ~
Whipstitching Worries (Book 9)
Needling Nemesis (Book 10)

Book Set 1
Includes Books (1-3):
Sewing Suspicion, Quilting Calamity & Pressing Matters
Book Set 2
Includes Books (1-5):
Sewing Suspicion, Quilting Calamity, Pressing Matters,
Threading Trouble & Stitching Concerns

Cozy Mysteries by Kathryn Mykel & P.C. James:
Senior Sassy Sleuths Series
(Short Stories, Shared Main Characters)
Senior Sassy Sleuths
Senior Sassy Sleuths Return
Senior Sassy Sleuths on the Trail

ADDITIONAL BOOKS

1950s Cozy Mysteries by Kathryn Mykel & P.C. James:
Duchess of Snodsbury Mysteries
Royally Dispatched
Royally Whacked
Royally Snuffed

Sweet & wholesome romance by Kathryn LeBlanc:
Home for a Hat Trick (Sweet Hockey Romance)
Christmas Star Cottage (Holiday Cottage Series)
Sugar Cookie Inn (Christmas at the Inn Series)
Quinn (Runaway Brides of the West Series)

Mail-Order Papa Series
A Banker for Bethany
A Carpenter for Catherine
A Lumberjack for Lorena

Honorable Husbands Series
Mail-Order Carpenter
Mail-Order Thief
Mail-Order Lumberjack

new heatherton series

A NEW QUILTING COZY MYSTERY SERIES

A crafty new series from award-winning author Kathryn Mykel stitches levity and suspense together with the charm of a fictitious small town on the coast of Maine, in this page-turning cozy mystery.

Be the first to receive exclusive information about the Heatherton Series here:
https://authorkathrynmykel.myflodesk.com/readernewslettersignup

Raining Quilts and Dogs: A Quilting Cozy Mystery

Read the first 3 chapters:
https://dl.bookfunnel.com/xjn5k680xg

Will the roof cave in on Elizabeth's new endeavor, or will she catch the murderer before she's basted?

Interior designer, Elizabeth Purdy has a notion to restore Saint Christina's Nunnery into a quilting retreat center but torrential downpours threaten to destroy the historic landmark before she even begins. When Elizabeth finds Heatherton's favorite neighbor and retired private investigator, Mr. Jenkins, murdered, face down in a puddle, she realizes that Mother Nature isn't the only villain on the loose.

With the deed and keys to the old monastery in hand, Elizabeth is in a race against time to pin down the culprit before tensions rise like the flood waters in this quiet, oceanside town. The quilters just wanna quilt, the neighborhood pets are barking Maine-iacs, and the town is completely cut off from their emergency services.

Support Raining Quilts and Dogs to uncover an unexpected crime today!

https://www.kickstarter.com/projects/authorkathrynmykel/raining-quilts-and-dogs

Quiltload of Trouble: A Quilting Cozy Mystery

Can Elizabeth clear her friends' good names before they're sent to the clink?

Elizabeth's efforts to restore Saint Christina's are stalled. With the help of her fellow Sip & Stitch quilters, she must pin down the murderer before the pressure bilges in their oceanside town.

Heatherton is buzzing with activity as the renovations on the library come to completion. The quilt raffle is sorely needed to help pay the final bills, but Councilwoman Kelly Kennedy is holding a grudge and wants the mayor to change the town's by-laws to ban gambling, including raffles. A local fisherman, Caspian, owner of the Seafood Shanty, hauls up a boatload of trouble, and it seems he's pulled in more than just the catch-of-the-day in his nets.

Will Elizabeth catch the culprit, or will the new mayor's fishy actions get them all in deep water?

https://www.kickstarter.com/projects/authorkathrynmykel/quiltload-of-trouble

Net of Deceit

Today, the air was charged with a sense of unease. The salty breeze from the Atlantic tugged at Elizabeth Purdy's fishtail braid as she stood on the edge of the docks, staring out at the restless waves. Heatherton's harbor was usually a scene of calm and routine, the steady hum of fishermen and the creak of boats blending into a familiar symphony.

Elizabeth adjusted her tote bag, filled with quilting supplies and half-finished projects from the Sip & Stitch group. The renovations at the monastery, Saint Christina's, had hit yet another snag, and she hoped to find solace in meeting with her friends. But first, she needed to make a quick stop at the Seafood Shanty to pick up fresh lobster for tonight's dinner.

As she approached the quaint, weather-worn building, she noticed a crowd gathered near the docks. Caspian, the rugged fisherman, owner of the Seafood Shanty, was at the center of it, his face flushed with a mix of confusion and anger. Elizabeth quickened her pace, her peach sundress with large white polka dots fluttered in the breeze. A new mystery was afoot. Her curiosity was piqued.

www.authorkathrynmykel.com/heatherton

Printed in Dunstable, United Kingdom